BEASTS AND BEAUTY

DANGEROUS TALES

ALSO BY SOMAN CHAINANI

SOMAN CHAINANI

BEASTS AND BEAUTY

DANGEROUS TALES

Illustrated by
JULIA IREDALE

HARPER
An Imprint of HarperCollinsPublishers

Beasts and Beauty: Dangerous Tales
Text copyright © 2021 by Soman Chainani
Illustrations copyright © 2021 by Julia Iredale
All rights reserved. Printed in Canada.
No part of this book may be used or reproduced in any manner
whatsoever without written permission except in the case of brief
quotations embodied in critical articles and reviews. For infor-
mation address HarperCollins Children's Books, a division of
HarperCollins Publishers, 195 Broadway, New York, NY 10007.
www.harpercollinschildrens.com

Library of Congress Control Number: 2021935419
ISBN 978-0-06-265263-8 (trade bdg.)
ISBN 978-0-06-314270-1 (special edition)
ISBN 978-0-06-315939-6 (int. ed.)

Typography by Amy Ryan
21 22 23 24 25   PC/TC   10 9 8 7 6 5 4 3 2 1
❖
First Edition

For Maria Tatar,
who opened the door . . .

Red Riding Hood   1

Snow White   18

Sleeping Beauty   46

Rapunzel   68

Jack and the Beanstalk   88

Hansel and Gretel   120

Beauty and the Beast   154

Bluebeard   182

Cinderella   208

The Little Mermaid   240

Rumpelstiltskin   256

Peter Pan   286

BEASTS AND BEAUTY

DANGEROUS TALES

RED
RIDING
HOOD

ON THE FIRST DAY OF SPRING, THE wolves eat the prettiest girl.

They warn the town which girl they want, slashing the door to her house and urinating on the step. No one sees the wolves, just as no one sees the dew before it sops the grass. As winter wanes, the town thinks the curse broken, seduced by the mercy of spring. But then the marking comes. Sometimes a few weeks before she will be eaten, sometimes a few days, for wolves decide on a prey in their own time. But once a girl is chosen, she is theirs. Neither child nor family can appeal. On the eve of spring, the wolves howl for their meal and the town marshals her to the edge of the forest and sends her in. Fail to deliver her and worse things will come than the loss of a pretty girl, though no one knows what these worse things could be. Soon the second howl echoes from the forest's belly: quieter, sated, the wolves' work done. The people disperse. The girl forgotten. A price to pay for time unfettered.

But spring lurks.

Another year gone.

Houses shudder, despite the haze of sunset, the sweet riot of blooms. A mother and father sit, lips cracked, nails torn, watching the girl as she gnaws the last meat off a bone, her russet hair dipping in the juice circling her plate. They didn't think she'd be trouble, born with spindly limbs, a pig nose, and peasant-brown skin, a muddy reflection of her makers. They were sure they'd have her for life. But beauty, like wolves, takes time to settle on its choice, a slow, cold horror seeding in a mother's heart. The girl's eyes deepen to sapphires, her skin shines like honey, her neck unfurls with the imperiousness of a swan—

Still, the mark on the door surprises her. She was ordinary too long. Beauty came like a malady. She hangs nothing on it, like it's paint to peel off. To die for such a trifle . . .

Stupid beasts.

She doesn't bother with fear.

Virtue is on her side.

She reaches for the knife on the table, the one her father used to cut her meat. The steel teeth slaver as she wipes it clean, grease spotting the cape she's knitted for the occasion. Red as blood, bright as fire. She's asking for it, wearing that in a forest. But there is no hiding from wolves. Might as well make it quick.

The knife heavies in her hand.

Where to keep it?

I need a basket for Grandmother, she announces.

Her mother says nothing.

Her father keeps eating.

Grandmother's house is across the river, the girl says. I'll send word once I'm safe.

Her mother gets up, holds her breath as she collects hard rolls, soggy fruit, acrid cheese. The father gives his wife a look. Food wasted on a futile mission. But there's no arguing. Not tonight. Besides, his daughter is as stubborn as his wife's mother, the kind of woman who expects a basket from a guest, even one running from wolves.

The sun douses with angry flares, a flame snatched in a fist. The wolves howl from the forest.

It is the first time the girl feels scared.

Until now, she thought she would beat them somehow. Human against animal. Good against evil.

But it is their song that stirs her—a dirge of self-pity, as if they cannot help themselves. They are prisoners of their nature.

And goodness is no weapon against the possessed.

Even so, she enters the forest calm.

The town brings her to the brink, every last man, woman, child, and they wait as she goes, hands clasped, as if praying for her soul. In truth, they are there to stop her from running back.

Her slippers crackle over twigs, a tentative path opening before her, the lane of girls sent to die. She remembers these girls, born beautiful, born marked, skulking furtively about town, avoiding the eyes of those that would sacrifice them. They knew, these sisters. Long before the wolves came. They knew they were meat.

The path narrows, trees snatching at her. She's used to paths closed off. It's not just the beauties who suffer. The other girls are tainted by the wolves too. The girls who weren't picked. Boys rake through them like leftovers. It's why any girl who marries one cleans up after him without complaint. She's lucky to be alive, they tell her in their grunts and growls. Lucky her beauty isn't worthy of beasts. Her mother was one of these, plucked from the scrap heap. The girl saw it in her father's face. All men spend their lives yearning for the one they can't have. The girl devoured by wolves. Now they're trapped with second-best. It's why her father is never happy. She would have married a boy much the same.

Not now though.

Whatever happens from here, her life will be different.

But a different life comes with a price.

It takes walking the path between life and death.

The knife lies hidden in the basket. A silver twinkle in her eye. Let them come. Just like that, they prowl out of darkness like fog, clouding the path where it ends. A tribe of formless shadows, like genies summoned to a wish. But it is their eyes that give them away, ruthless yellow crescents as old as time. She raises the red hood of her cape like armor, backs up—

Moonlight traps her, the forest's torch.

They circle. Boys in breeches of black leather, their chests bared, their forearms taut with veins. For a moment, she thinks this is all a ruse: that there were never wolves, only boys marking a girl for themselves. A girl to run with their rebel tribe. A princess for wayward princes . . . But now she sees their lips coated with drool, the trail of hair down their bellies. She smells the feral musk.

This is the problem with wolves. They are tricksters. Shapeshifters that draw you close. Killing you is not enough. They want to play with you first.

Your choice, speaks one of the boys, dark-skulled and long in the tooth. His words are wet yet plaintive somehow, an unusual plea.

Then she sees the hunger in his eyes. In all their eyes.

Now she understands.

She must choose which wolf will eat her.

That is the game.

Play along, she thinks.

Survival comes not in resistance to the game but in winning it.

She takes her time, evaluating each, while her

hand slides into the basket, feeling for the knife, her eyes roving up and down their lean, famished ribs, as if they've starved the whole year for this moment. But there is one who is different. He, the leader of the pack, hidden in the shadows, arms crossed, chest full, the one who isn't famished at all, who frankly looks bored. He has pearl-white skin and dark unruly curls, like he's Cupid himself, his beauty so unmatched by the others that he knows he will be picked, just as he has always been picked before. But there is no conquest in this, his eyes say. He sees the ugly duckling inside her, beauty found instead of earned. She won't taste as good because of it. Pick someone else, he's telling her. He's had his fill. But it is no use. For he is beauty incarnate. Which is why he knows she will choose him.

And she does.

Go, he tells the others.

They whine but do not fight, limping into the trees.

They'll have the scraps, he tells her.

She is alone with him now. He looks her over. The cold yellow eyes warm to gold. His pale cheeks fleck pink. With the other boys gone, he's considering her anew. He stands erect. Saliva sops his mouth.

Then he sees her hand in her basket.

She squeezes the knife.

Either he hasn't spotted it or he isn't bothered.

Be my guest, he says. Eat your little picnic. Fatten yourself up. You'll only taste better.

It's for my sister, she replies. She lives across the river. With Grandmother.

His ears twitch.

River's past our territory. Don't know the girls who live out there, he admits. Nothing but skin and bones, I bet.

Not true, the girl sighs. My sister's more beautiful than I.

The dots of pink in his cheeks expand. Younger or older?

Younger.

Across the river? Where?

She chuckles. As if I'd tell you that!

He lunges, snatches her by the throat. Your grandmother's house. Where is it. Blood rims his eyes, foam flying off his lip. *Tell me.*

Or what? You'll eat me? says the girl. You're

already going to do that.

He lifts her off the ground, over his dripping jaws as if he'll swallow her in one gulp. But it's not she that he's dripping for.

Tell me and I'll let you free.

She considers this. And your friends?

They'll follow me the moment I go. You run back home and kiss Mommy Daddy. Now tell me before I change my mind.

She pauses. Wolves lie.

So do girls too big for their britches, he snarls, his claws cutting into her neck. Could be making this all up so I free you.

Blood trickles down her throat. It doesn't stop him. Nothing will stop him. He will make her tell him, no matter what tortures he has to invent.

Follow the river around its east banks, she says. Her voice a crushed whisper. There's a willow grove. Cross to the other side and you'll see a cottage in the glen.

He drops her hard to the ground, then kneels over her on all fours, his face and chest turning hairier, hairier, his voice a hot-mouthed hiss. If she isn't there, I'll find you and rip out your bones. Mommy Daddy too.

He slashes his claws across her cheek to mark her.

Then he starts to run.

Soon, she hears the scamper of wolves caught unawares, loping after their leader.

Relief.

So much relief as she hustles away. Not because she's free. Relief because she isn't beautiful anymore, her cheek carved up, the sign of a girl who strayed from the path. She can imagine her mother's and father's faces upon her return, first joy, then pity, for who would want such a girl—the town's offering, sent in sacrifice, sent in submission, but too willful to play the part. Bad Girl, they'll whisper. Broke the rules. Other girls might get ideas. No, no, no. Better to be eaten by wolves. Even her mother and father would agree. Only it's not her mother and father she's going to see.

Grandmother's house is a short distance to the west. Wolves run quicker, of course, but she's sent them east, around the river, which even at the fastest pace will take a fair bit of time. She pries between trees, tangled in darkness, but the fear is gone. She takes time to marvel at the forest: the jackknife of branches, the kiss of the underbrush, the blinking jewels of eyes in the dark. Red, hooded serpents rear their heads at the blood-colored girl slithering past. It is not enough for the wolves to rule this kingdom into which they are born, she thinks. They want more. A suffering of innocents. A thrill of entitlement. A plunder of something they're not meant to have.

Careful, she reminds herself, sensing she's slowed. A ravenous male moves faster than a girl thinks. Soon she hears the burbling of water. The river batters her gently as she fords the shallows, fish catching in the tail of her hood before she lets them free. Through the hickory grove and past the fern field lies the red-leafed clearing and the old wood cottage, its two small windows moonlit like glowing eyes, the eaves coated in gray moss like fur. She's only been to Grandmother's house a few times and the last long ago, but still she remembers the way, like a cat that knows the way home.

Knock, knock.

She does it quietly, in case the wolves have spies.

Knock, knock.

The door opens.

Grandmother's there, her face a shriveled prune, her bee-colored hair hacked short. She has a fat scar under her eye, her mouth twisted in a scowl. She takes one look at her granddaughter, sniffs at the wounds on her cheek.

Come inside, she says.

Follow the trail of spittle through the willow grove.

A ring of wolves surround the house, backs arched, teeth gnashed, starving for the scraps their leader promised. They are tired, resentful of a fine meal given up. They would revolt if they had the spine.

The leader bides his time, rising onto two feet,

shaking off dirt as his fur recedes, combing his
Cupid-curl hair as he approaches the door, the perfect gentleman caller.

The door is open for him.

He enters lightly. His pale, hairy feet scrape
along the floorboards. He isn't used to working for
his supper. He isn't used to being upright. But there
is thrill in it. Pretending to be tame.

A fire casts a watchful glow over the room, spit-
ting sparks at him, snap, snap, snap. The house is
old and stale, nothing worth noticing. A thick old
broomstick. A bluebird clock out of rhythm. A
blanket over a lump on a rocking chair. An empty
basket on a table. Some crumbs of cheese.

But it is the bed in the corner that is fresh and
full, a figure shrouded in milk-white veils.

Who's there? she says.

Your prince, says he.

Come closer.

He obeys, his mouth silvery wet.

My . . . what wrinkled skin you have, he says.

A witch's spell. Better to hide my youth and
beauty. Come closer.

But what cloudy eyes you have, he says.

Better to see into a prince's soul. Come closer.

But what shriveled lips you have, he says.

Better to kiss my prince with and break the spell.

The veil of the bed falls.

The boy kisses old Grandmother's lips, thirsty for his reward.

Yet no spell is broken.

Instead, old bones crack. She cackles in his face. Laughs and laughs and laughs. She sees what he really is. An impotent beast.

His eyes go jagged. He bares his teeth.

The mask of a boy shamed.

She knows what that means. He'll kill and kill until he's drunk. Until he forgets what he's done. One leap and he's on the bed, skin become fur, boy become wolf—

Should have checked that rocking chair!

The knife impales his heart, and he spins in shock, faced with a girl in a hood red as his blood, more beautiful than he remembered.

His cry sends the other wolves running in, but they are too starved to fight. Grandmother bashes them with her broom, snap, snap, snap.

Together, they fall, these wicked changelings,

howling to their death.

But triumph and disaster often ring the same.

Far away, villagers leave the forest, trusting their sacrifice complete.

Each year, a new girl is marked. Her door slashed with warning.

On the first day of spring, she hears the wolves call. The villagers marshal her to the forest. She kisses Mother and Father goodbye. Quavering, she goes into the dark. Follows the path like she's told.

But at the end of the path there are no wolves.

Instead, she finds a house filled with girls just like her.

Beauties who've left beauty behind.

An old woman brings her to the table.

Girls gather round. Join hands like a pack.

The old woman smiles beneath her red hood.

She was a girl too, once.

Together, they raise heads and howl.

SNOW
WHITE

A GIRL MARRIES A WEAK MAN.

He says the right things at the right time, a prince who promises her happily ever after. So many see only her skin, how different she is from the fair maidens of this land. They treat her like a lump of coal, like black is a sin. But this prince makes her feel beautiful, something she's never felt before. When he rides her to his castle, he carries her over the threshold, to a bedroom pure and white.

The people are suspicious though. So is the prince's father. His son marrying a girl like her, when there are so many other girls to be had? But everyone keeps their resentments to themselves. It is the polite thing to do.

Until the king dies.

Now the prince is king, his princess the queen. And the people don't want her to be queen. They can only hold their tongues for so long. The young king feels their venom. The queen does too, but the king takes it personally. Love is his privilege. He's not used to fighting for it. So he doesn't. Instead, he keeps little company with his queen and strays about the kingdom with women fairer than she.

This reassures the people.

Midwinter brews, harsh and lonely. In her room, the queen sits by the window, sewing and watching white snow fall in imperious, suffocating little sheets. A crow settles near her, and the snow attacks, whiting out its feathers until it's a dove. The queen shudders. Her needle pricks her finger, spilling blood onto the bird.

If only I had a child, she thinks. A child that's mine to love. White as snow. Red as blood. Black as a crow.

And she kisses the bird to seal her wish.

Soon afterward, she gives birth to a girl with crow-black skin, blood-red lips, eyes with whites as bright as snow.

She calls her Snow White and laughs.

And oh how she loves the child, made exactly like she's wished, even though the king treats the girl badly, for there is nothing in her that reminds him of himself. So, too, do the people of the kingdom, who look upon the girl like a curse. The queen keeps her close, warding the child like a jewel, for only in her keeping can she teach her how to be loved.

But then illness comes for the queen, the way snow came for the crow, and by winter's end, she is no more.

A year later, the king marries anew. She has milk-white cheeks, a brown tumble of hair, and eyes as sharp as a bear trap. This new queen has no love for Snow White, a stain on the family, and puts her stepdaughter to work cleaning the castle. Not that the queen wants a child of her own. A child might take the sheen off her own rose. Instead, she bears a magic mirror on the wall in her vast, echoing chamber, and every morning she asks:

> *Mirror, mirror, on the wall,*
> *Who's the fairest one of all?*

The mirror always replies:

> *You, O Queen, are the fairest of all.*

Her eyes soften, her skin gains color, relief swells at her breast, a feeling she calls happiness, because for a moment, what she wants to be true and the truth are one and the same.

Snow White keeps growing though, and so does her beauty, even if it's stowed away in toilets and kitchens, even beneath a white coat of flour and dust. Her stepmother has forgotten about her entirely, the girl put in her place, until one day, the queen asks her mirror:

Mirror, mirror, on the wall,
Who's the fairest one of all?

The mirror replies:

My queen, you may think yourself the fairest,
But Snow White is a thousand times more fair.

At first, the queen scoffs. A girl like Snow White . . . *fair?* But then she remembers the mirror had named the queen the fair one all these years, and if she trusted the mirror then, she must trust the mirror now. No one else in the kingdom would consider the idea, of course. That Snow White is more beautiful than her. Beauty in this world has rules. But what if Snow White breaks these rules? What if other people start to see what the mirror does?

From that moment on, she hates Snow White even more, doubling her chores, making her sleep in a closet, berating her husband if he gives the girl a second glance. But it isn't enough. The more she keeps Snow White down, the more envy and jealousy snake inside her, as if her heart knows something she doesn't, as if she willfully denies a higher law than her own. The girl is the blind spot in her reflection. Day or night, the queen doesn't have a moment's peace.

Summer swelters the palace like a greenhouse. In heat, the queen's hatred blooms wilder and grows teeth. It is not enough to keep the girl slaved and out of sight; now the queen kicks and mocks her, baiting her to rebel, like a fly to a trap. The girl holds her tongue. She knows a nemesis when she sees one. A nemesis uses any excuse to kill you. Your life drains theirs of power. There is no escape now. Fate has bonded them: the stronger the one, the weaker the other. And Snow White grows stronger every day.

The mirror confirms it.

Snow White is a thousand times more fair.

Again, again, again.
Now the queen knows. The girl can't be beaten.
So she must die.
A huntsman is called.
Take the girl into the forest, the queen says.

Bring me her lungs and liver after you've killed her.

The huntsman doesn't argue. He has a wife and two sons to feed, and the queen pays well.

But when he takes Snow White into the woods, she doesn't flee. Nor does she cry when he pulls the knife from his belt and raises it at her chest. Instead, she stares him in the eye and says: For what?

No one has ever asked him such a thing. Most about to die run for their lives as if they are guilty.

The huntsman lowers the knife.

Hurry off and never come back, he grunts.

Into the tangled wood she goes, and the huntsman sighs. The animals will kill her by dawn, but at least it won't be his doing. He waits until a boar comes close and he stabs it mercilessly, extracting lungs and liver before taking them to the queen. All things under the skin look the same. The queen sniffs them, hunger licking at her heart. She orders the cook to boil the gifts in brine and she devours them, thinking she's drunk the girl's body into her own.

A privileged child cannot survive in the forest. The vines and brambles would reach out and strangle them. The animals would eat them, sup, sup,

sup. But Snow White isn't privileged. She hasn't lost touch
with her nature. Her beauty
is the beauty of the trees, the
flowers, the foxes. It cannot
be rivaled with a powdered face
and well-groomed hair. It is why
the queen sends someone else to
kill her. To kill the girl herself
would be like glaring into the sun.
But the huntsman errs in thinking
the forest will devour her. Instead,
the bears and wolves make way, the
healthiest fruits dropping at her feet.
She runs and runs, a creature of the
night. Past the river, toward the edge
of the queen's kingdom, white-capped

mountains pointy and high, one, two, three. Then, in a spot of moonlight, a cottage appears. It is so clean and quaint on the outside, with a white picket fence and white petunias and a neatly pruned lawn, that there is little threat in slipping up the path and knocking on the door, nor in pushing it open when no one comes. But inside is a surprise—a riot of earthy colors and luxurious smells and gem-crusted candles and cozy rugs and blankets. The palace was a mausoleum, but this is a home, with seven plates on a table, small clay circles, each with its own cracks, seven small knives and forks beside them. There are seven cups too, along with jugs of honeywine. In the kitchen, there is a pumpkin pie cut into seven pieces and mud-dusted greens heaped into a pile. Seven small beds line the wall, each with a pair of slippers at its foot. She makes the greens into a salad, spritzing it with lemon and oils from the cupboard, then helps herself to a piece of pie and a full cup of wine.

It is time to leave now, she thinks. To stay here is danger. But she tells herself this while she curls up in a bed not her own and falls deep into sleep, the way she once did at her mother's breast.

It is well past dark when the owners of the cottage return, seven dwarfs who spend their days in the queen's mountains, mining for gold and digging for gems in deep, dark caves where the queen's miners never deign to go. Whistling up the path, they enter the house, seven lanterns lit, and all at once, they see someone has been inside.

Who drank our wine? says one.

Who ate our pie? says a second.

Who made a salad? says a third.

But it is the eldest dwarf, with the longest beard and tiredest eyes, that gets to the point: Who's in my bed?

And they all shine their lanterns upon Snow White, who is so used to sleeping in the shadows that she springs up at once.

It is the first time she's seen anyone as black as she, seven little men with onyx skin and lily-white beards and colorful tunics capped with matching hats. In the palace, no one looked like her, which she'd thought didn't matter, since skin shouldn't matter. Who cares if others judged her for it? Those who saw her only for her skin were themselves blind. But now she sees she was blind too, that without her mother, she had no mirror, no reflection, no proof that she was made well to hold in her heart, like a black swan in a flock of white that's told it's a mistake instead of a pearl of pearls. And it is this lie that made her silent all these years because she thought the answer was silence, instead of mining for words of protest, words trapped heavy inside her—but here, facing these strangers, she sets them free, telling the story of a vile, vain queen who bamboozled her father and tried to kill his daughter because she was threatened by her beauty, even though Snow White never felt beautiful at all.

The dwarfs look at each other.

This is why we live by ourselves, the eldest dwarf grumps.

Tears rise to Snow White's eyes. I didn't mean to trouble you, she says, hurrying for the door.

Where will you go? asks the eldest.

Beyond the mountains, the girl says.

That's where we came from, the dwarf sighs. King out there doesn't want people like us. You won't be safe.

Snow White doesn't know what to do. This

world isn't made for her, even though she was born into it.

The dwarfs confer, mumbling and grumbling, before the eldest raises his head.

Do you know any good bedtime stories? he asks. We like fairy tales. If you tell us fairy tales, you can stay.

Snow White smiles with relief. You'll have every tale I know, she says.

Even though she doesn't know any fairy tales. Not any good ones. All the stories she heard at the castle about beasts and beauties don't make the slightest bit of sense. But she's too smart to admit it or to say there are no fairy tales for people like them. Instead, she thinks: Now it's time to make some.

An eighth bed is made.

The next morning, the dwarfs go back to the mines, but not before the eldest issues Snow White a warning: Beware your stepmother. If she is as you say, her heart is black. And black hearts don't sleep quietly in white castles. Sooner or later, she will come for you.

Snow White takes heed, but forgive her for

worrying about something other than her stepmother for just a while, especially with a bedtime
story to write and a supper to make, for the dwarfs
have put her in charge of that too, given the savor of
her salad the night before. But she isn't aggrieved by
either task. When so many of your years have been
spent in vigilance of life or death, to be preoccu-
pied by thoughts of recipes and a proper moral for
a story seem like a luxury once afforded to people
other than her. Her stepmother isn't too far from
her mind though, and the dragons and trolls and
ogres that Snow White invents in her tales, tor-
menting dark, valiant heroes, all have the queen's
colorless skin and bear-trap eyes.

Meanwhile, at the castle, the queen dreams of
Snow White's lung and liver and wishes she had
some more. At first, she avoids her mirror, because
her soul is at peace and she is once again the fairest
in the land. Plus, she wants the mirror to know she
can live without it, especially since it spent so many
days touting a name not her own. But soon enough,
an unease claws at the queen's chest, like a hand
creeping out from a grave. There is only one cure.
To the glass she goes—

Mirror, mirror, on the wall,
Who's the fairest of them all?

The mirror grins as it replies:

You think you're the fairest, my dear queen,
But it is Snow White, who lives with seven dwarfs
In a cottage at mountain's edge
That is the fairest one of all.

The queen has little reaction to this news. It was as if she knew the girl would haunt her, like a ghost from another life. That Snow White is far away or nesting with dirty dwarfs is no solace. Her mere existence is a threat to the way the world is, an omen of what it might become.

She has a plan though. Women like her always do. Kill Snow White and kill her well. This time, by her own hand.

The queen stews bat dust, snake tongue, and toad blood into a potion which she drinks with a gasp, clutching her throat as her face blackens beyond black and sags off her bones, like a mockery of the beauty her mirror called fair. The magic continues down her spine, draining her strength and soul. When it is done, she is barely alive. Then she dips a set of combs into poison and goes into the forest.

At the cottage, Snow White is plotting her latest tale about wicked witches and the disguises they wear, while she coaxes her bread to rise and hums a lively tune.

Combs for sale!

A craggy voice outside.

Combs for sale! Combs to make you beautiful!

Snow White answers the door.

The old peddler is stooped to a hideous squat with burned-looking skin and a leering, hungry gaze that reminds her of a wolf's. For a moment, she wonders if it is the queen come to kill her, but even Snow White can't imagine her stepmother debasing herself like this. Crisping her skin to ash? Wrinkling herself to leather? Skulking from the palace into dwarfs' petunias? The queen wants her dead, but even she wouldn't sink so low. Which means the girl takes pity on the peddler and buys all three combs with a few loose coins from the dwarfs' coppers.

Let me comb your hair, the peddler says. Make you beautiful.

More a command than a wish.

Snow White thinks of the way the queen used to mock her hair at the castle, taunting that it needed combing and straightening and was best put up in a rag.

Those days are gone. Snow White's hair grows free.

But the memories remain like scars.

All right, Snow White says.

The queen digs the comb in her scalp and the poison seeps in. Snow White realizes her mistake. She falls dead into white flowers, her face wax-pale.

Best she's ever looked, thinks the queen, hobbling away.

Soon after, the seven dwarfs return home, only to find Snow

White crumpled on their doorstep. Luckily, the eldest spots the footprints away from the girl's body and smells the bitter haze of black magic. It doesn't take long for him to find the poisoned comb and yank it out, using a pond leech to suck the venom. Her cheeks color, her breathing sputters back, and eyes flicking open, she starts to tell the story of an old, sweet peddler who wanted to make her beautiful, only to turn wicked at a moment's turn . . . but then she sees the dwarfs' faces and knows how foolish she's been.

At the palace, the queen spends the night brewing antidotes to restore her beauty but still frets that she's been left darker than before. The mirror has something to say though, this time unasked.

Fair as fair can be and still not enough, dear Queen,
For Snow White is still alive,
And the fairest ever seen.

The queen's heart electrifies. Alive! Still! What a monster. Respect for the girl builds in her heart. Beauty who fights like a beast. But if the girl thinks she's winning, she's well wrong. She'll just be killed again and again until her spirit is broken. This is the thrill in the queen's heart. That she gets to plot the girl's murder a third time. That she gets to destroy her as ritual. In ugliness, the queen has found herself.

Out comes the bat dust and toad blood.

Across the forest, the eldest dwarf pokes Snow White with a broom when she's too busy fussing over her bread loaf to pay attention—

Don't open the door for anyone, he repeats. You hear me?

Mm-hmm, says Snow White.

The eldest tramps his dwarfs out to the mines, quite sure the girl has no sense and will welcome the next friendly witch who comes her way. On this account, he is right.

A few hours later, the voice croaks outside.

Apples for sale! Fresh apples!

No answer at the cottage.

Knock, knock, knock.

Big, juicy apples!

Nothing.

One-of-a-kind apples! Fit for a queen!

The door opens—

Well in that case, Snow White says, a bread loaf between oven mitts.

Her eyes lift, and she almost drops the bread.

Her stepmother has once again hexed her face black, but an unholy black, the kind of black that has no name, because it is white turned inside out, an inversion, a distortion, like a mask or a slab of paint, a misunderstanding of what skin is and how deep it goes.

I have an apple just for you, dearie, coos the peddler.

Just like you had a comb? Snow White asks.

Mmm? Comb?

The one you sold me yesterday.

Mmm, must be confusing me with another, says the peddler.

Ah, Snow White thinks. We're playing that game.

Well, a peddler sold me a poisoned comb and I nearly died, so I can't be taking things from strangers, she explains.

Poison! A sweet girl like you! Oh dear, I'd never do such a thing! the peddler insists, drawing forth a luscious apple. Here, I'll even cut it in half. You take the red half. I'll take the white.

She bites into the snow-white fruit and sucks the juice off her lips. Mmmmm. Here . . . eat up.

The girl doesn't take her half.

What does it cost? she asks. You never said.

Whatever you can pay, the peddler dismisses. A coin or two.

I don't have any coins, says Snow White.

The peddler frowns: But yesterday— She catches herself, thrusts the red half at her. Take it for free then.

For free? Snow White scoffs. Coming all this way into the dark of the forest to sell your one-of-a-kind apple for nothing? Now, that would be suspicious. I have to pay you. How about some bread? A bit black on the outside, but inside, pure white just like your part of the apple.

The peddler practically pushes the red half into her hands. Really, just have a taste before it dries up—

You sure you don't want a try? says Snow White, glancing at her loaf. I bake a special butter into the bread. Butter that makes you fair and lovely.

The peddler's eyes shiver. Oh?

Let me give you some, says Snow White. Make you beautiful.

Oh . . . well . . . The peddler stiffens, having forgotten all about the apple, limp at her side. Just a small taste, maybe.

Snow White tears off a piece, holds it to the peddler like a mother bird to her chick.

The peddler snatches it, swallows it whole, eyes closed like a girl courting a fairy's spell. Strange, she murmurs, such a bitter taste . . . like something I've known—

Her eyes flare open, fly to the girl.

Snow White waits like a storyteller who's found the right ending. For she's baked the cursed comb into the bread and killed the queen with her own poison.

Down the black-faced witch falls into white flowers.

Snow White pries the apple from her hands so that it won't leave seeds to sprout and burns it with the bread in the fireplace.

When the dwarfs come home, they aren't sure what to do with the queen's body. This becomes especially nettlesome since her magic potion has worn off, returning her to her high-boned pallor. Snow White favors bringing the queen's body to her father, the king, but the dwarfs say that will lead to both Snow White's and the dwarfs' deaths, no matter how good their intentions. One look at the girl and the dwarfs and a dead queen, and the people will demand their heads. To seek a fair ending for their kind is as foolish as it is noble. Better to avoid an ending altogether.

So the dwarfs put the queen in a coffin made of glass and hike her to the mountains and leave her there at the steepest peak in the hopes someone will claim her. Each day, on their way to the mines, they give her a passing glance, doffing hats and bowing heads, because it's the respectful thing to do in the presence of the dead.

Seasons come and go, birds make their nests upon the glass, the coffin becomes part of the mountain itself.

Then one day, when the dwarfs have almost forgotten about her, they see someone waiting by the coffin when they reach the peak.

A prince.

Tall and handsome with frost-colored hair.

The son of the king on the other side of the mountains. The same king who drove the dwarfs out for the color of their skin.

But the prince shows no ill will to the dwarfs. Instead, he beholds the glass-bound queen.

So beautiful, he says. Surely the fairest in the land.

The dwarfs stifle a groan. He's one of those.

But it is the eldest who sees something in the prince's eyes — a spark, a tinder, the possibility of something different.

Not quite the fairest, he says.

The prince looks at him for the first time.

Oh?

The dwarf whispers to a nesting bird, sends it to the cottage.

The prince returns to gazing at the queen like a hypnotized child. Only when he sees a stir in the glass, like magic in a mirror, does he snap from his trance and turn.

Snow White stands there like his reflection.

The prince is so undone he falls back into the queen's box, knocking it off the mountain.

A girl marries a weak man.

He says the right things at the right time, a prince who promises her happily ever after. So many see only her skin, how different she is from the fair maidens of this land. They treat her like a lump of coal, like black is a sin. But this prince makes her feel beautiful, something she's never felt before. When he rides her to his castle, he carries her over the threshold, to a bedroom pure and white.

The people are suspicious though. So is the prince's father. His son marrying a girl like her, when there are so many other girls to be had? But everyone keeps their resentments to themselves. It is the polite thing to do.

Until the king dies.

Now the prince is king, his princess the queen. And the people don't want her to be queen. They can only hold their tongues for so long. The young king feels their venom. The queen does too, but the king takes it personally. Love is his privilege. He's not used to fighting for it. So he doesn't. Instead, he keeps little company with his queen and strays about the kingdom with women fairer than she.

This reassures the people.

Midwinter brews, harsh and lonely. In her room, the queen sits by the window, sewing and watching white snow fall in imperious, suffocating little sheets.

If only I had a child, she thinks. A child that's mine to love. White as snow. Red as blood. Black as a crow.

Soon afterward, she gives birth to a girl with crow-black skin, blood-red lips, eyes with whites as bright as snow.

She calls her Little Snow White.

And oh how she loves the child, made exactly like she's wished, even though the king treats the girl badly, for there is nothing in her that reminds him of himself. So, too, do the people of the kingdom, who look upon the girl like a curse. The queen keeps her close, warding the child like a jewel, for only in her keeping can she teach her how to be loved.

But then illness comes for the queen—

Not this time.

Seven dwarfs steal her into the forest. Dwarfs who make her fight for every breath. Dwarfs who nurse her with their love. Dwarfs who protect her, like a vain queen protects her beauty. Snow White doesn't die, even though she's supposed to die.

The doors to the castle are thrown open.

She is back, stronger than before.

The king startles, the story thrown off-script.

Snow White glares him in the eye.

Her child won't lose her mother.

Her child won't be kept down.

Her child will be raised right.

A black swan that knows it's a queen.

Mother hugs child to her breast and mounts her throne.

Hair wild, feet to the earth.

Black that shines brighter than gold.

No, she's not going anywhere.

SLEEPING BEAUTY

TO THE PRINCE, IT WAS CLEAR: demons were drinking his blood.

There was no other explanation.

No way of explaining how a boy of sixteen could wake each morning with his head pounding, his skin clammy and pale, and blood dripped across his sheets. No way of explaining how small, red-rimmed wounds punctured his neck, bicep, and chest. No way of explaining how he dreamed of faceless forms on top of him, feasting on him . . . only to wake with his shirt torn open and no one there.

At first, he went to his father, the king, but no father wants to hear the torments of his son's bed-chamber, especially demons that go against God. Insistent, the boy bared his neck, showing the cursed marks, prompting the king to send the doctor, who probed the boy with rods and steel and confirmed the king's suspicions: Needs a wife.

At this, the boy went to his mother, confiding in her the pallor that afflicted him, the bloody handprints that stained his sheets, the haunted ghosts of his mornings . . . but the queen knew no good would come in believing him.

So it continued, the prince afraid to sleep each night, eyes wide and vigilant for his foe, only to smell a strange rush of roses and stir awake, shirt ripped, sun-kissed like a sleeping beauty, sucked of blood once more.

The wounds in his skin healed in time, replaced by fresh ones, roving up and down his body. He was a prisoner to the demon, who neither showed its

face nor seemed to want anything more, no bargain or sacrifice or ransom, only to drink from
the sleeping prince. Soon a dark shame filled the
prince's heart, especially when girls began to vie
for it. For he was at the marrying age now, with
eligible females paraded before him each morning and afternoon as he sat sallow and ravaged, his
father and mother beside him, jurors to a pageant
of beauty, gifts, and talent. There was the Princess
of Sarapul, who brought a hundred cherry blossom
trees; the Countess of Khorkina, who reached her
head into a tiger's mouth; the Marquesa of Sal-
timbanca, who did a dance of veils that seduced
the men into sleep . . . except for the prince, that
is. He stayed wide awake, even as the marquesa
writhed and whirled, the bells on her anklets jingle-
jangling. She swung her hips and did the splits; men
moaned and dropped into sleep, the prince numb to
it all. Seeing his father snoring and the dancer well
pleased with herself, the prince feigned slumber so
as not to be rude. A cruel irony, of course—against
the demon, sleep caged him ruthlessly; but facing a female's charm, he batted it away like a soap
bubble. Why had the demon chosen *him*? Why no

one else? Then again he couldn't be sure; he'd had moments, with page boys or men in town or even the odd knight, where he'd seen the same haunted pallor, the odd-placed scarf or upturned collar that seemed to be hiding something, the same frightened eyes he saw in the mirror each morning, as if they too had caught the malady without cure. . . . But then he put the thought away. He was the only one. He was sure of it. The demon had picked *him*. Yet, the more he considered it, the more he seemed the wrong choice. The kingdom was teeming with wanton dukes, corrupt priests, spiteful traitors; even the prince's father made no secret of his taste for women and drink. The prince had been a good boy, God-seeking and hardworking and disciplined in mind and deed. That he would be the devil's toy was unfathomable. So what could be wrong with him? A defect in the blood? A kink in his soul? Whatever it was, he had to be rid of it. So he prayed harder, thought purer, gave his courters his fullest attentions as they peacocked and preened. And yet, still the smell of roses came, the horror of morning, with more blood drunken out of him, the wounds deeper, deeper, deeper, tempting him with the reprieve of death, but never giving him over.

And so he set a trap.

A solid ring, with razor-steel teeth, hidden in the sheets where he slept.

For two nights, the demon didn't come, as if it knew it was tempting fate. But on the third night, at the peak of dark, the prince smelled the roses—

A cry yanked him out of sleep.

Something was on top of him.

Not a demon or monster.

Instead, a boy about his age.

He had red waves of hair, a long, gentle nose, and skin the color of the moon. He clutched his bloody wrist in the folds of his shirt, his mouth quivering, his eyes bright with fear.

A severed hand lay in the trap.

Blood leaked onto the prince.

Blood for once not his own.

The prince and thief locked eyes.

A broken-winged bird, caught.

Then flying—the thief for the window, gasping, trailing red, the prince lunging after him.

But he was gone to the night, a part of him left behind.

In the spring, the prince chose a bride.

There was no reason to delay. The night crimes had ceased, his sheets clean again, the mornings reclaimed with vigor and promise. Everyone spoke of how strapping the young prince looked, his skin rosier, his chest proud, as if whatever had been afflicting him had been cast out and replaced with a woman's love.

Even so, his pick for a wife was surprising: the Contessa of Tagheria, who for all her beauty, had a glacial air and forbidding manner, like a statue too valuable to touch. Where the other rivals competed for the prince's hand, the contessa simply claimed it, insisting that they should be married by the end of spring and the prince offering no objection, as

if he'd been yearning for a soul to captain his fate.
The king thought the prince should have a girl more
lively; the queen thought he should have one more
humble; but given their son was no longer speaking
of demons in the night, they ceded their blessing
without fuss.

And yet, as the wedding neared, the prince's glow
doused, the sleepless pallor returning. At night, he
lay awake in his bedchamber, gazing at the window
he'd left wide open, wondering what became of the
boy who'd feasted on him. When sleep came, it
came fitfully, filled with dreams of severed hands
and bloodless hearts. It was these spells in the night,
raising heat and chills in his flesh, that became his
real life, where the days became a somnolent haze,
his bride eager to involve him in the wedding plans
and the prince returning vacant looks, as if to a
stranger.

Soon the contessa's own gaze sharpened, a
snake's losing sight of her prey.

So she proposed a trip.

A twelve-day tour of neighboring realms that
would show off their love, filled with grand parades
and sumptuous state dinners and white-tie balls, a

glittering tribute to the couple that would impress upon the prince how awaited their wedding was and how much was at stake. A marvelous idea, clapped the boy's father, who thought some time in close quarters with his bride might restore his son's puff. Soon the bags were packed, the couple sent on their way, no expense spared. And though the prince still wore a heavy-lidded melancholy, he satisfied the contessa's wants at every turn and gave no window to his own. Indeed, he asked only one thing of her, a peculiar request that took her by surprise—that at each stop, he be arranged to meet any townspeople missing a hand. It was an easy wish to indulge, especially since the prince's mood improved markedly in greeting these unfortunate souls and bestowing sacks of gold upon them. That he was wasting treasure on maimed people he didn't know rankled the contessa, but she made no sign of her displeasure, other than an off-hand question as they rode out of Ravenna.

What interest do you have in them? These folks you ask for?

The prince remained silent, his eyes fixed out the carriage window, as if he'd left something behind.

Plenty of people suffer in life, she snipped. It is their fate. A lump of gold won't bring back their hands.

The gold is so he shows his face, the prince replied briskly.

He? his bride asked.

The prince didn't answer.

He? she repeated.

Her groom paused a long moment before he turned to her.

A thief used to come in the night to me. I took his hand with a trap. Now I wish to return it to him.

A thief in the night, the contessa said, the words tart in her mouth. And now you wish to reward him?

Not reward, said the prince. Only to give back what's been taken.

From a *thief*, his bride repeated.

The prince returned to his window. He'd made a mistake in telling her. Especially since she watched closely now as he continued his meetings in each new realm, the contessa hunting for any signs he'd found the one he'd spoken of. But the prince's stares stayed blank, the gold meted out and the wretched dismissed, until at last they returned back home, the contessa content that the prince's quest had gone unfulfilled.

Or so she thought.

For back in Ravenna, he'd found the thief, though he almost hadn't recognized him. A henpecking pair had rushed the boy forth, an obsequious couple with greedy eyes, clearly intent on the gold their son had reaped them, while the boy receded, clutching the stump at his wrist. He scarcely looked the same: his cheeks sunken and cadaverous, his muscles poorly fed, nothing like the wicked cupid who came to drink from the prince by the moon. Now the prince and boy locked eyes once more, the boy cowering into the shadows, as if the light of the sun might burn him to ash. Every step the prince took toward him, the boy's father and his ogreish wife obstructed, cooing and flattering to solicit more gold, praising the prince's size and strength and virility, until the prince had enough and dumped the bag of coins into the street. Stooge and crone dove, scavenging every last one, as the prince bent toward the boy, slipping a note in his shirt, which told him to come to the Forest of Edan on the twelfth moon.

For it was on this twelfth night that the prince and the contessa were married, the gardens of the castle aglow with crystals and lights, thousands of high-ranking revelers packed amid the orangerie and mirror pools and Neptune fountain, the king and queen seated in thrones like overlords, keeping track of who greeted them with the most obeisance, while dukes and counts fawned over the newly wedded contessa, uncowed by the ring on her finger. No one paid attention then, when the groom slipped off into the forest surrounding the palace and found the thief from Ravenna waiting for him, just as he'd asked.

Neither spoke a long while, the boy hiding his scarred arm.

Go on, then, he said at last, puffing up. Kill me. That's why you're here, isn't it? Finish me and go to your bride. No one will notice I'm gone.

The prince reached into his coat, and the thief shuddered, knowing he must take his punishment.

Instead, the prince brought forth the boy's lost hand.

He held it into the moonlight, at once offering it to him and keeping it close, as if it belonged to them both.

The thief didn't move, even as the prince came closer, closer.

Patiently, the prince took his arm, firm and tight, and fitted him with the missing piece, their shadows twined, like two sides of a moon.

Tears sprung to the boy's eyes.

They spilled to the ground, sprouting a bed of roses.

The scent drugged the prince, his eyes rolling back.

He woke with a start—

A spray of blood in the forest, his shirt slashed away, new wounds in his flank.

Now he returned to his wedding, a wildling of the night, chest bared, blood spattered, roses ripe in his hair, and yet, now everyone was drawn to him where they weren't before, his father kissing him while revelers drew close, sniffing and slavering at the prince, then bowing at his sides, like dogs of a pack to a wolf.

The contessa noticed.

She noticed too when he built his own tower in the castle, higher than any others, with only a single window carved out of its stone, and the entrance to the tower sealed with gilded doors, carved every inch with roses.

His princess wasn't given a key.

That the prince would want to be walled off from his wife riled the contessa, but there was no one to appeal to, given the king took great pains to avoid his own wife and other than the usual public appearances, the king and queen stayed fortressed in separate wings. Still, there was something sinister about a handsome buck, in the prime of youth, taking no notice of his spouse, even as she swanned about the castle in Chantilly lace and diaphanous silks. But leave beauty spurned too long and just wait: beauty turns to beast. The contessa stationed her own guards outside the prince's tower, scouring the night for his visitors, but none came. She put two more high in a tree, commanding them to watch the prince's window, but each time, they'd fall asleep and wake at dawn, only remembering a strange smell of roses. So she suffered in furious silence, her face haggard; her hair ragged; her eyes, once brilliant gems, now hard, cold stones. All the while, the prince emerged from his golden spire each morning, glowing like a cloudless sun, despite sleepless creases under his eyes and hot red wounds in his skin.

If only she could be content with diamonds and champagne. That's why she married him, after all, for the gowns and the boots and the fame, and these bounties of a princess still flowed plentifully to her. But pleasure is only a fleeting respite. With each morning that the prince looked happier and happier, rage fizzed in the contessa's heart, a craving to punish him for the happiness she hadn't given him permission to have. Soon, the contessa began to feel the stirrings of black magic, the calling of a witch, for what is a witch but a princess who no longer has need for her prince.

In the depths of night, the contessa went to the doors of the prince's tower, his rose-carved vault, and taking a knife, slit her hand, smearing her blood on his doors like a wolf marking a kill. Overnight, a dark spell took hold, a spiraling twist of thorns, thick and purple, the color of strangled love, binding the tower from top to bottom and shrouding the window in the thorns' teeth, like the trap once kept in a prince's bed.

At last she slept soundly, sure her prince's joy had been snuffed out, but the next morning there he was at the breakfast table, two wounds fresh near his unbuttoned shirt, his smile a blissful crescent, directed aimlessly toward her, as if he hardly remembered why she was there.

Outside, thorns had turned to roses.

No more magic, she decided.

She'd take care of things herself.

The worst kind of witch.

That night, she waited until the prince kept himself in his tower. Then she sharpened a carving knife in the kitchen and climbed the rose vines to his window. Into his bedchamber she went, the prince asleep and splayed against white sheets, a half smile on his face, a beauty waiting to be kissed awake.

Not tonight, the contessa thought. She cut his throat with her knife, then climbed down the roses, tiptoeing back to her room with a maleficent grin.

The next morning, she joined the king and queen at breakfast, still smiling to herself, relishing the sugared toast and strawberry crepes, letting the syrup dribble down her chin, waiting for the screams from the tower once the maids did their rounds.

Instead, at the stroke of nine, the doors to the dining room opened and the prince entered, humming softly to himself, his gaze on his wife, a ring of roses around his neck, precisely where she'd slashed it.

The contessa jumped out of her chair, eyes

aflame, a red scorch in her cheeks, her blood boiling so deep from the inside that she let forth a murderous scream and dashed her foot against the stone floor, again and again and again, until it shattered beneath her and she plunged straight through to her death.

The king and the queen went on eating their toast, for these were the kinds of things that happened between sons and wives.

In the days that followed, the prince brought the Ravenna boy to take her place at the table. Across the boy's throat was a jagged scar, like one made by a carving knife, the same width and size as the ring of roses around the prince's neck, as if they'd traded beauty and pain. The king and queen looked upon this boy with moon-white skin and wild red hair and asked him no questions, nor did the boy offer answers, and indeed, as long as nothing was spoken, there was peace and tranquility, a family as it should be. But then one day, the boy wasn't there, his entry to the castle barred.

I need a grandson, the king told the prince. He said it in much the same tone he once told the boy that he needed a wife.

The prince stared at the chair across from him. The boy missing.

You will be king one day, his father insisted. A king must have an heir.

The prince's eyes stayed on the empty chair.

Give me an heir and my guards will leave your window unwatched, the king promised.

Now the prince faced him.

If only fathers invested in love as much as they do in sons, he said.

He retreated to his tower and never came out, not for meals, not for court, not for any of the beautiful girls sent to his tower, eager to give the prince an heir. Furious, the king sent guards to seal off the prince's window, but each night, the men smelled a charge of roses before waking to a bright, clean sun and the bloodstained sheets that maids brought forth from the chamber. Night after night, season after season, roses and blood, roses and blood, like a marriage rite, the prince and his caller unseen, until the king gave up and sent the guards away, leaving his son to his shame.

Then one day, something strange happened.

A maid was changing the sheets, stripping the

usual marks. But when she turned back, the blood was gone, and in its place, a child.

A baby boy with rose-red hair.

The king came running the moment he heard, thieving the child away from the prince before dropping him in shock—

He bites! he said.

As the child did to the queen.

But it was to the prince that his son caused no pain, and he lived with him there in the tower, shut away from the world, except for the thief that came through the window each night to watch over them both until morning, like a visit from mother moon.

RAPUNZEL

BEWARE THE PARENT WHO CRAVES A child in order to mend a broken heart.

They often come with the best of intentions, as this one does, with his once rose-red hair turned gray and his sagging flesh and hump in his spine, a man once a boy, whose parents kept him in a tower and smothered him with love, hoarding him away, until it was too late to find love for himself. Now he longs for a child of his own, but he knows he would love it too much, the way his parents loved him, so instead he tends a garden that has become his world. The cabbage and leeks and beans. The bluebells and harebells and foxgloves. A garden he culls and controls, yet it doesn't resent him. Instead, it thrives as he dotes upon each sprout, nursing it big and strong until it's time to snip it short and sell it for coins. But there is one thing in the garden not for sale: the rapunzel, greenest of greens, which blooms in crimped, coiled braids, the kind of braids his father would make in his hair when it spun too long, the hair that now has gone thin, leaving patches against his oily skull. He loves his rapunzel the most, which he lets grow and grow, twisting and turning upon itself, like a broken spinning wheel, like a crooked spire to the moon, before at last its life is over, and it wilts and falls, a reminder that the thing he loves cannot be protected and this is why he must not have a child. But for now it is enough, rapunzel, rapunzel, rising and falling again and again, life and death in a braided tower, the one true love of his heart.

Then a woman is hungry.

She lives overlooking the garden, in a handsome chalet, with three floors and two maids. She has everything she could want—a husband, a house, a child in her belly—and yet still it won't suffice, not when the rapunzel is there, so lush and scrumptious, and yet grown only to die. She glowers at the scrawny figure skulking in the garden, hooded robe, craggy stoop, slimy eels of hair. What kind of witch blooms such a garden only to kill its most

beautiful prize? That she confuses the man for a
witch is unfortunate; if she'd known it was a man,
she would have asked him herself. But all she sees is
a witch, so she tells her husband to sneak over the
wall when the moon is high and steal the rapunzel for her. Her husband knows full well to stay
away from a witch's garden, and besides, such crav-
ings pass. But not this one, for it is more than the
rapunzel his wife craves—it is the love the witch
pours into it, love she wants to feel for herself and
eat and taste and consume into her belly, where her
baby now lies.

Don't you see? she tells her husband. I must have
it. And if I don't, I will die.

Men don't know
what to respond to
such things.

So the next night, he slips into the garden after the witch is gone and steals a handful of the twisted greens, not enough for his wife to be satisfied, but enough for its absence to be noticed. When the husband slaves back for more, the witch is ready and pins him down in bluebells, a knife to his throat. That the witch is a man only scares the husband more. He begs for his life, for the wife he's left at home, so that the unborn child in her womb shall have a father—

He's said too much.

He sees it in the man's eyes.

This witch wants the child.

Even if it will be bad for him.

Even if it's not his child to take.

And yet, he's already given it a name.

Rapunzel.

The husband isn't as committed.

He makes the deal: the child for his life.

As he tells his wife, he had no choice.

What can she do? She's tied to his fortunes.

If he dies, she will too.

So it's done.

The child is born.

Then taken and spirited away.

Left behind is the garden, growing over walls, into our homes, wild and thirsty for love.

There is a misconception that a girl who grows up in a tower dreams of the outside world.

How can she dream of something she does not know?

She is fifteen now. How quickly the years go, when each day is the same, nothing to hold on to, no memories to make. When she looks out her window, she sees nothing but shields of forest and the moat of thorns beneath her bower. Her hair is the only way to tell time, the plaits shiny and smooth, the color of a golden egg, each week braided a little bit longer by her father, until it is as long as the tower itself. When she was younger, she used to ask why she couldn't climb down and roam free like Daddy did, why she couldn't run the edges of the forest with the pigs and dogs and goats she'd glimpse scampering in and out, why she couldn't pick the wild roses between tower and trees, but then her father would come back with buckets of roses or a piglet or a puppy or a goat, and she learned that whatever she wished for outside her tower he would deliver inside it, like a storybook fairy. With each year, the gifts grew more extravagant: crystal-sewn gowns of mulberry silk, mille-crepe cakes with vanilla cream, potted orchids and gloriosas, a menagerie of birds and cats and bunnies to join the hog and poodle and goat already grown old. Where these things come from, she doesn't know; each day he ventures into the forest and returns with new treasures, her once humble chamber now a palace of marabou rugs and lambswool blankets and rich soaps and creams, until she's so cozy and sedated that she doesn't think about going out anymore, only about what gifts he will bring. Besides, didn't Father once read her that story about a lad named Jack who climbed a beanstalk to steal treasure? And wasn't the moral of the story to let men do the business of thieving from giants? She has embraced the laziness of being spoiled, the sweetness of being the apple of one's eye. Her only toil is the twenty minutes it takes for him to climb her hair when he comes home, prompted by his breathless shout—*Rapunzel, Rapunzel, let down your hair!*—as if afraid she won't answer to her name, as if afraid today, her ropes of gold won't come. She takes advantage of this, of course. Each time, she waits a bit longer before she unravels. And yet, there is always relief when he calls, for he makes her feel like a princess, even though she is just a girl without much to do.

But something's changed.

She has less patience with his doting now, as if the ritual has grown old, but there is nothing to take its place, nothing to move on to. She snaps at him, he sulks, she repents, the two bound by this strange quarantine they used to call love. She looks at herself longer in the mirror now, lingers in the bath under the bubbles, puts on lipstick for no one at all. Her sleep is sweaty and rough: shadows climbing out of night, cuffing her to bed with her hair. At first, she's scared when these dreams come. Then she misses them when they don't. Her father has insisted that there is nothing to discover in the world; that anything she desires he can manifest. Now she suspects that he lies.

He holds on tighter. She can see the way he

watches her, like a hawk tracking a rabbit that might get away, his hard-eyed reflection caught in the mirror as she gleans her own beauty. For the first time, she is taken with someone other than him. That she is the source of her own pleasure offers him no solace. When she sings out the window, he barks at her to be quiet, as if a neighbor might hear. When he climbs her hair, he claws and yanks at it as if it belongs to him. Each yearns for something more, something they don't have words for, their souls only giving clues but not the courage to name it, so instead they cling to each other, ball and chain, in this prison of their own making.

Then one day he dallies too long, and when the birds come to her window, asking for a song, she sings into the sky unfettered, her father not there to rein her in.

A voice—

Rapunzel, Rapunzel,
Let down your hair!

It is deep, serene, with no spikes of warning. It doesn't sound like her father. And yet it must be, she sighs, squinting into dusk's inky abyss. He climbs her hair with more grace and care than usual, as if afraid to hurt her. Oh no, she thinks: he's trying to be nice. To make her think their home is a happy one. Suddenly, she wishes she'd left him. That she'd packed a bag and escaped. But how to get down? Where to go? She has these thoughts every day. Right in this moment as he comes home. Only it's too late. Maybe tomorrow. Her father rides over the edge—

She recoils in surprise, onto the stone floor, her hair whipping around her neck like a collar.

This man is not her father.

He looks near her age, maybe a few years older, with soft brown skin, smoke-gray eyes, a wide, strong nose, and a thick, smiling mouth. He has a gold ring in his right ear and a shaved, square head.

Who knew someone could be beautiful with so little hair?

Her pets make no effort to guard her from him. Fear or sloth.

He tells her he's the Prince of Aneres. That he's heard her singing on his rides through the forest and has been watching her for weeks, waiting for a time when her keeper stayed out too long, so he could lure her into letting him up instead. She hardly hears a word he's saying, entranced by the horse hairs on his sleeves and the sword strapped to his belt. Only when he falls silent does she realize he's a stranger. That she hasn't summoned him from the shadows of dreams.

What do you want from me? she asks.

So many things, he says.

He looks around the chamber, the overstuffed comforts, the overrun plants, the overfed pets.

But most of all to take you away, he says.

My hair is the way down. For you to go, I must stay, she says.

Then I shall come every day until we find a way together, he vows.

She has no answer. None in words, at least. Her body pulls closer, as if it wants things from him too, even if she doesn't know what they are. But in the stillness, she knows what to do, her lips reaching up as his bend down.

Such a strange thing, a kiss, she thinks. Who made it? But then there are no more thoughts, not until their mouths part.

I want more, she says.

He smiles. Tomorrow.

Then he's gone, the sound of hooves punishing the earth in smooth, even claps, until it's quiet, like a storm passed.

Father returns and he's wary. He sniffs and prowls about, like a dog sensing threat. He doesn't notice the boot print by the window, which her goat scuffs out, or the horse hair on her breast, which her cat laps up. (Not fear or sloth, it turns out, but hope!) Still, her father knows something's wrong, and he berates her for her untidy hair and smudged lipstick, and as he sleeps, strangling his pillow, snoring hotly, she wonders if he can smell kisses.

The prince returns the next day.

Before she can get her fill of kisses, he wants to talk.

My guards and I have a plan to rescue you, he says. Tomorrow you'll come away with me.

To the ends of the earth? she breathes.

To my castle, he replies.

Oh, she sighs. Another tower.

A much bigger one, he insists, on bended knee, sword flashing at his hip. You'll be my wife. A prince's wife. Like the girls in storybooks.

She looks down on him. Her father never read her storybooks like that. All the tales he told her were about good girls who stayed home while the men slayed monsters.

Tell me about being a wife, she says.

You live in my palace with servants and maids and courtiers at your every whim, he answers.

the gates of a new realm,

bright as a pearl in sunlight,

endless as a whirlpool that has no

bottom.

Mmm . . . pretty sure that was just
a reflection of the storm. Waves, rain, lightning . . . Even I'd be fooled.

I wouldn't expect you to understand, the mermaid sighs.

And why not?

Because you're a witch.

Says who?

245

Says everyone. Look at this place: a lair of bones on the far side of the swamp pools where nothing lives, surrounded by polyps that snare anything that tries to pass, filled with potions and cauldrons and shelves of things only a witch would have: frog toes and snake tongues and mermaid blood . . .

Then why did you come here if I'm a witch?

Because they say you can make wishes come true. And I need to be with my prince.

And what would your daddy say if he knew you were here? With a *witch*?

Other mermaids have come to you for help and died for it. I see their skeletons in the sticky weeds around your house. I know your price is steep. But true love is worth any cost. My dad wouldn't understand. He believes marriage is about finding someone your parents approve of. In his eyes, a girl should be quiet and obedient. To be honest, Daddy would never think I'd come here. He wouldn't think any of his daughters could come here. Because we all know how much he hates you. You're his mortal enemy.

Well, that's a bit dramatic—

He says you're vain, petty, greedy, and a bitter

Sounds oppressive, she replies.

You have dresses and diamonds and riches you've never dreamed of. Gifts of the world, bestowed by visiting emperors and kings.

I have riches here, and I don't have to dress up for others to get them, she says. Besides, who wants gifts from people they don't even know? Sounds insidious.

A prince's wife helps him lead his kingdom to peace and prosperity, he says sternly.

Sounds exhausting, she yawns.

He stands up. What is it you want, then?

To run free in the forest in my nightgown and dance in the rain, she says.

She likes how riled he's getting. But it's the truth. Every time it rains, it's all she can think of. What it must feel like to not be sheltered from it. What it feels like to get wet.

Only madwomen do that, he admonishes. Not my wife.

Yesterday she would have gone wherever this man told her to.

No thank you, then, she says.

He stares at her. What?

I don't want to be your wife, she says. I just want your kisses.

That's not how it works, he scolds. To be kissed, you must be a wife.

What nonsense, she puffs. You're only my first kiss. Surely, I have to try others too. Besides, how do I know there aren't better ones out there until I have more of yours?

His face is red now, as if he isn't used to parrying with girls. If there's one thing she's learned from living with a man, it's that men need to be reminded of their place.

But this one won't yield.

He's looking at her the way she looks at him.

Each thinking the other is for sale.

Do you know how many girls want to be my bride? he growls.

It seems their price is very low, she says.

He simmers, his once lovely lips now gnarling into a sneer. For a moment, she's reminded of her father.

You've been alone too long, he says, striding for the window. Tomorrow, I'll return and you'll change your tune.

No need, she says. I'll wait for a prince who has no price for his kiss.

There is no such prince, he promises.

Oh? Let's see how far my song carries, then.

He lashes back: If a prince kisses a girl who is not his wife, then she is no princess. She's a *witch*.

I thought you said there is no such prince, she reminds him. To make the case of *if* means there must be some. And besides, you kissed a girl who is not your wife, and on more than one occasion. So it appears you already have a taste for witches.

She licks her lips at him. Wonder what that makes *you*.

Blood flushes his face. His eyes blaze fire. He grabs his sword from his belt and with a single step, he lunges at her and slashes her hair, again, again, three times, hacking it so short it looks like fur on a goblin's head. See who kisses you now, he snarls—

Goat, pig, dog ram into him, a menagerie of guardians, and he goes tumbling out the tower, hair tangled around him, plunging him into the bay of thorns.

When Father returns, he finds a boy blinded, thrashing in the briars, bound by his daughter's locks.

Tears fill Father's eyes.

Good girl, he thinks.

Good girl.

Stay away! A witch in the tower! the boy raves, hearing him approach. Stay away!

Father leans over him.

Not a witch, he soothes. My princess.

His tears fall into the boy's eyes, healing him, bringing back his sight.

The prince takes one look at him.

And runs.

There is no way up to her.

The braids are in pieces. The golden rope undone.

She is up there, and he is down here.

So he plants rapunzel beneath the tower. And so does she, up in her spire, in a pot by the window, the tendrils blooming toward the earth.

Little by little his vines look for hers and hers look for his, growing strong from both ends, month after month, rapunzel, rapunzel, until two halves touch.

Now it's ready, the bridge complete. Father goes up and daughter comes down, before they meet in the middle, soaked in midnight rain, like a perfect Ever After. He clings to her, precious Rapunzel, and at last he wonders if it is enough, this love she's grown to reach him, this love that might finally fill the hole in his heart. Then he opens his eyes and he's holding nothing but twisted greens, no one else there, and as he looks out at the great garden of night, he sees a shadow dancing free into rain, like a stolen spirit on the way home.

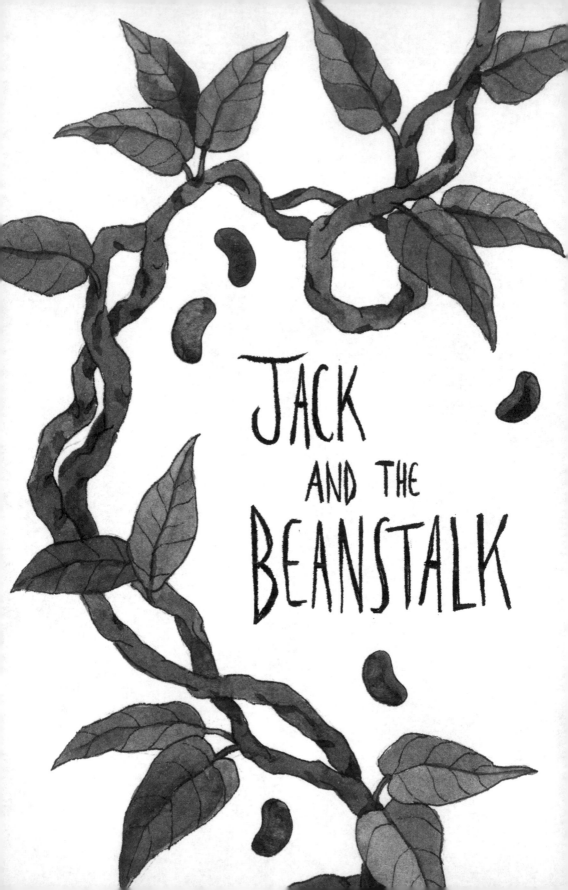

WHAT TO DO WITH A BOY LIKE JACK?

Fourteen years old and still expects his mother to butter his bread. How idle his days, shooting marbles and making up songs and staring at clouds, the only rise coming when he spots a pretty girl pass and puffs up his chest, only to have his mum bunt her head out the window and shout: Jack, go milk that good-for-nothin' cow!

Off he goes to the barn to pump the udders of Milky White, wishing he had his own house, where he and Milky could live together, instead of here where they have no respect. He doesn't like his mother, mostly because she doesn't like him, and he dreams of making something of himself and stuffing it in her face, because wouldn't that be a happy ending, proving the person wrong who treats you like nothing? And yet, he can't wean himself off his mother's toil, as if the less she thinks of him, the more he clings to her, eating her food, sapping her hot water, tromping muddy boots in and breaking her things like a plundering giant, until she stops trying to keep the place nice, for what would be the point?

Naturally, she blames the father, for it's a father's duty to whip Jack into shape, and the man was as useless as the son. He idled about the streets, jawing at strangers and badgering them for coins, trying to drum up change, only to go and lose it on dice, whereby he'd gamble greater sums he didn't even have, leaving him in perpetual debts to men smarter and more sober than he. Only at the peak of the moon would he slosh on home, pumped full of drink and crooning of all the treasures he'd buy when his luck turned round. Before his wife could smack him, he'd foist her a kiss and remind her: Ain't I the one who got us Milky White on a strong roll of dice? Ain't I the one who made you a son?

And what could she say, for both things were true. And what could she say when he'd coddle Jack and tell the boy he had his dad's God-given charm and that boys like Jack married beyond their means, just like his father had. That too was true, for Jack's mother was once the maiden Alina, a lovely, hardworking girl who every boy in town wanted for a wife, but she chose Jack's father because he was as handsome as he was slothful, and she thought, May as well marry a handsome one because sloth's something you can change. Learned her lesson, didn't she! Watched him loaf off with every dime they had, his debts growing bigger and bigger, until one day, his debtors came for him, five burly shadows in the doorway like the specters of giants, who marched him away and never brought him back. That's what you get for marrying a man you think you can change. Now she's poor and alone and stuck with his son, who's as hopeless as his father, and there'll be no changing the lad either.

It was obvious what happened to the man, of course, and the widow thought Jack knew full well his dad had been sunk in the swamp or dumped down a hole, and the boy would heed the warning and scare on the rightful path. Little did she know, he'd spun his own tale—Daddy wasn't dead at all but whisked to a land high in the sky, where he'd been crowned king—and by the time his mother tried to imprint him with the truth, it was too late.

That's what he *wants* you to think, Jack would say. As he tells it, his dad had found Happy Ever After, free of his wife's claws, and now was counting riches in a faraway castle, waiting for his son to join him.

One day, he'll come back for me, Jack insists. You'll see.

The widow can only grit her teeth and keep buttering the boy's bread, for it is clear he'll be even more of a fool than his father. No doubt about it: Jack will live with her until they're both old and gray. For what girl worth her salt would marry a boy like that?

As she sees it, he has hardly any charms at all. Those gooey green eyes, perhaps, and his crooked grin and that mop of brown hair he keeps blowing out of his eyes, puff, puff, puff. But his clothes are always rumpled and his shoes untied, and he lopes about on long, skinny legs, his bottom wagging, as if no one's taught him the proper way to walk. How she nags and grouses at him, but Jack knows there's no arguing with her, so he bottles up everything he wants to say and takes it out to the barn and tells it to Milky White instead. And the old cow listens dutifully, once a pure, young thing, won in a dice match from a perfectly good home and brought here to graze in a half-dead yard, underfed, no room to roam, until she's nothing but a lazy bag of bones, yielding a few spurts of milk each morn before she keels over with a fart and yawns back to sleep. But oh how Jack adores her, cuddling to her belly like she's his real mother, one that doesn't judge or scold or yell, and in return, he sneaks her half his supper most nights.

If only you cared about me as much as you do that cow, Jack's mother gripes. You'd get a job. You'd earn your keep. You'd make something of yourself.

Milky White thinks I'm something, Jack replies.

One day, Milky White will go dry and we'll have to sell her for coins. See how much she thinks of you then, his mother snaps.

But Jack just chuckles and pipes, Milky White is a magic cow and magic cows never go dry.

Well, what can you say to that?

But then, of course, comes the day where Jack

goes out with the milk pail and slinks back without a drop to drink, not in the morning, not at noon, not at night, while Milky White curls up and waits for her supper, though she's done nothing to earn it. And still Jack loves her like she's a prize even without milk, and this sets his mother into a storm, for this was the way she'd doted on his futile, feckless father, until he'd ruined them both.

Enough.

Time for the boy to grow up.

The next morning, she nooses the cow with a heavy rope. We're selling Milky White, she says. I'll take her to the butcher, score ourselves a decent sum.

Jack cries: No! I'll get a job! I'll work night and day! I'll do anything!

Go and try it, his mother dares.

And he does. But no one wants him, not the blacksmith or the miller or the baker, for they'd known the father, which means they know the son. Only the street sweeper takes pity, offering two farthings for a day's work, scooping up dung from horses passed, but Jack lasts only till lunchtime, the smell and ache weakening his resolve, along with thoughts of Dad in his skybound castle, counting all the gold that could be his son's.

So it is done, the widow wrangling the cow out the door, ignoring Jack's pleas, ready to haggle her price.

Let me do it, Jack pleads, blocking her path. Otherwise she'll know where she's going. She'll get too scared.

This, the widow can't deny him, for she'll have to live with the boy long after Milky White becomes meat, and she needs him to make his peace with it.

Go quick, then! she puffs. But no less than ten silver pieces for her, otherwise you're in for a thrashing!

A long walk for a last goodbye. The boy and his magic cow, the one who'd run out of milk but never run out of love, cozying side by side along the soft dirt road that runs from the cottages to the market square. Every few steps, Milky White looks at Jack with cool, glassy eyes, but he just kisses her on the nose and scratches her ear, as if they'll be together till world's end, where his father waits in fields of gold.

Milky White knows better. She smells the

butcher miles away.

But as they draw closer, Jack notices a woman on the side of the road. She's posed in the weedy grass, arms folded over her half-cut white blouse, her colorful skirt swaying. Her skin is a rich, smooth brown, her lips dangerous red, her eyes speckled with green. Gold hoops cuff her wrist and dance from her ears.

Sweet baby, she says, gazing at the cow. Some animals have old souls.

That's my Milky. Good ol' gal, Jack touts. Gonna get ten silvers for her.

The woman frowns. Ten silvers? Oh no. No, no. She's worth much more than that.

She strokes Milky White's ear. Sell her to me. I'll take good care of her. She won't be served on any man's plate.

Jack stiffens. And you'll let me buy her back when I get the money?

If your price is as fair as mine, she says.

What will you pay? he asks.

From her pocket, she draws five tiny pods, green as emeralds. They quiver in the sun.

Beans? he scoffs.

Magic beans, she says.

Pssh, he starts, but she's leaned in now, hand on his back, lips at his ear—

Plant them in your garden and they'll grow high into the sky. Higher than the clouds. New worlds await, your troubles behind you.

He looks at her, her eyes hypnotic, her breath so sweet.

Dad, he thinks.

At home, the widow is out of butter. Her bread is dry.

He bolts into the house like a prisoner out of jail, no cow at his side.

Good boy, his mother sighs. How much did you get for her? Ten? Fifteen?

He thrusts out his palm, the beans dull in dying light. Magic beans! They grow into a—

He doesn't have time to finish. She thrashes him until the sun comes down and sends him away without a bite to eat.

Jack weeps on his bed. The beating knocked some sense into him. Fifteen years old soon. No cow, no lass, no respect, and a bunch of dumb beans. What a fool. That woman must have taken one look at him and known he'd be hers for the taking. He thinks of Milky White. Maybe she has a good home now. Or maybe that woman sold her to the butcher herself. Poor old cow. He failed her like Dad failed him. There ain't no palace in the sky, just like there's no magic beans to ease his troubles. His mother is right about him. She's always been right. He flings the pods out the window and shoves his head under his pillow. Tomorrow he'll go back into town. Tomorrow he'll go back to sweeping dung, head held high.

Most days, a spear of sunlight wakes Jack with a stab in the eye, followed by Milky White's loud moos, demanding her morning feed so she can slack back to sleep. But today, there is neither, no devilish sun and no grievous cow, only a thick coat of dark that keeps him cozying in bed until he's well full of rest and rolls over with a yawn, glancing out the window at the giant beanstalk that's grown in his garden.

Jack falls out of bed.

He's putting on his pants as he scrambles outside, never a good idea, which sends him tumbling onto his face in a patch of mud. Slowly, he lifts his eyes to the thing in the sky, a colossal green pole the width of two elephants, twisting into the clouds, far beyond what he can see. His mother is there in the garden, the neighbors too, all of them shielding their eyes and frozen still, peering up the beanstalk, as if waiting for something to come down or someone to go up.

Me, Jack thinks.

It has to be me.

Because it was him who earned the magic beans.

Which means the woman who took Milky White told him the truth. And if she told the truth about the beans, then that means she told the truth about . . .

Off he goes, leaping on the beanstalk like a lizard flying for harbor, his hands gripping the veiny ridges, hoisting himself up.

No, Jack! his mother cries, but it's half-hearted, as if he's someone else's problem now.

Measure by measure, he climbs, the smell of the beanstalk so ripe and full and fresh he can feel his heart swell, like this is what life should be, big and untamed and mysterious, nothing like the bollocks old town he's left behind. He's famished though, after so much exertion, plus starved of supper and breakfast, but still he persists, clouds gathering round, birds pecking at his rump, unsure if he is friend or foe. Only once does he falter, his feet slipping, his body falling, before his hands catch a vine, and for the first time in his life, he feels his luck has changed.

At last, he reaches the top, a firm green frond linked to more green fronds, like a maze of giant lily pads into a hot, wet jungle, where everything seems twice the size it should be, the trees, the rocks, the flowers and fruit . . . He sets his sights on a meal, then hears a mighty roar and spots elk and lemurs sprinting past, giving him spooked looks that say there's no food to find because you *are* the food, and now Jack is running, even though he doesn't know who he's running from or where he is running to—

Then a house. Bigger than any he's ever seen before. Or taller, at least. It's high as a castle, the

wood moldy and green, with two wings off the main, the windows all shut up. It looks like a sleeping gargoyle, snarled in toothy branches, as if the jungle has sprung around it. The knocker on the door is solid gold, a monster's face, which gives Jack pause, but then he hears the roar again, more animals scampering, and he raps on the door, clap, clap, clap. Jack wipes his face, blows at his hair, puff, puff, puff. But no one comes. Jack knocks again.

This time, the door opens.

Jack's stomach twists.

Dad?

For it looks just like him, with a bushy brown beard and a thick mane of hair and a crinkly forehead, only he's thinner, much thinner, no cushy potbelly or big soft chest, just bare bony legs that poke out like sticks. He doesn't seem to recognize Jack at all, screwing him with a firm-eyed stare.

I ain't your daddy, he grumps. Too busy to be a daddy, caring for the missus and all. Best be runnin' along before she's back, 'cause then there'll be trouble. Skit skat.

He starts to close the door, but Jack jams his foot in.

Please, Dad. I'm hungry. Can't you give me something to eat? Just enough to get me on my way.

I ain't your daddy, the man repeats. And this time Jack knows it is true, for his glare is too cold. Jack backs down, retreating out the door—

Then something in the man's face changes, as if he doesn't want to be rid of him yet.

Lad your age shouldn't be skin and bones, he growls. Come in before the missus gets home. Feed you a bite and send you back where you came. Quick, quick! Skit skat!

He holds the door open, waving the ruffian in, but Jack doesn't go in, he goes straight at the man, who shirks back in surprise, but it's too late—the boy is hugging him, a big, giant hug, not his dad, not his house, but so close, oh so close, and for a boy like Jack, close is well and good enough.

It is a strange and barebones home, with more space than things, but Jack doesn't get much of a look, glimpsing only the high ceilings, a few birds nested in the bower, and the hint of a bed much bigger than his own, before the man leads him to the kitchen and points sternly at the table and chair.

Jack sits and watches the man shuffle about, pulling ingredients from the overstuffed pantry, mumbling about how his whole life is spent in the kitchen and how he wants to get away but this is his lot in life and lots don't change.

Definitely not his dad, Jack thinks, for Dad knows nothing about a kitchen, and besides, Dad would have been chuffed to see him, like he'd been each night coming home from the pub, reeking of beer and meat and hugging Jack so hard he thought his bones might break. But this dad didn't hug him back and is all prickly and gaunt where Dad was cuddly and soft, and Jack wonders what kind of wife would let a man get like that.

A few plates plop down, and while Jack's been busy thinking, the man's whipped up pancakes with syrup, a pileful of bacon, and three eggs runny at the sides. It's a full feast, and Jack hasn't seen a feast since the few times his mum tried to reward his dad after he got a job at the mill and stopped his drinking and acted all respectable-like. That didn't last long.

Jack eats so much that his tummy is a tub of sugar and grease, his mind a pleasurable fog, before he notices his host seated across, squinting hard at him.

Aren't you going to eat? Jack asks.

Missus don't like me to eat without her, the man says.

Missus ain't here, Jack points out.

What happened to your daddy? he asks.

Disappeared, Jack says. He pauses, thinking it over. Killed, actually. Racked up too many debts.

His host frowns. Leaving a young lad behind, that's no good. Least you got your mum, right?

The boy sighs. Can't do anything right enough for her.

Sounds like my missus, says the man.

A stomping in the garden —

At least that's the sound, like thunder hitting ground, the whole house rattling like an echo. Plates shudder out of Jack's hands, shatter on the floor; he whips his head to his host, afraid of another thrashing, but the man's out of his chair, rearing Jack by his armpits, before he stuffs him in the oven and shuts the door. Jack puts his eye to a crack in the stone, the man dashing about, helter-skelter, sweeping up Jack's mess—

Fee fi fo fum,
I smell the blood of a little one!

The roar rattles in Jack's ears. It is a voice of rage, like a soul emptied out, closer, closer—

Be he alive or be he dead,
I'll grind his bones to make my bread!

The doors to the house crash open to the black sole of a bare foot, so big it would crush anything beneath. In comes the missus, ten feet tall, with a suffocating smell, like fetid earth, her skin blackish green, her dark hair roped with leaves and twigs and maggots. Maybe once she had a human face, this giant come to roost, but now it is a furious mask, her raw eyes bloodshot, her yellow teeth gnashing, her fists like two stones. Jack's only seen monsters in storybooks, but here's one in the flesh, real as can be. And yet, the way she blows into the house, a storm cloud of doom, misery incarnate, it's

strangely familiar, like he's known it before.

There is a boy in this house! she shouts. A bony, good-for-nothing boy who no one wants! I smell him in every nook and cranny! Husband, boil him for my breakfast!

Jack's heart shrinks. He didn't know you could

smell things like that.

Nonsense, it's just your undergarments. Need washing, her husband replies. What did you bring from your hunt?

The giantess pulls a white calf off her belt, still alive and strung by the heels, and throws it down on the table. Roast it up, milky and white! And clean up this house, you bum! So dirty I'm smelling boys where there ain't none!

Yes, love. Now sit and count your gold while I make your breakfast, her husband says.

That the ogress does, as Jack frets in the oven, about his good-for-nothing smell, about the sweet calf to be butchered, about being trapped in a giant's house. But then, as the ogress counts her bags of gold, she falls asleep at the table, snoring so loud the whole house shakes once more. Quick, the husband opens the oven, lets Jack out, and gives his bottom a shove toward the door, before the man huddles in the pantry, hunting spices to cook his wife's calf. Jack knows he should leave at once and leave empty-handed; it's the right thing to do, what a good-for-something boy would do. . . . But sometimes, there are bigger things in life than what's right. He grabs the calf under one arm, a bag of gold under the other, and off he goes, past the sleeping giant, out the house, to the beanstalk, fast as his legs can carry. Down, down, down, he goes, and when he reaches the ground, at the peak of sun, there are his mother and neighbors, right where he'd left them, earthbound in his giant shadow, as Jack hugs the calf to his heart, empties the bag of gold in a blinding glint, and stands atop the hill like a dragon, glowering down at his mum to pipe: Now what do you have to say about *that?*

A few months later, his mother is back on his case.

For a while, there was hope. He was famous in town, lovely girls jumping at the chance to have a date with him, duck breast and chocolate soufflés at Le Gavroche, while Jack regaled them all with his tales of escaping the giant, hoping to get a kiss. But a bag of gold goes quick, especially with a calf to feed and his mum adding a new wing to the house and buying herself sleek leather boots and head-to-toe fox furs, her own dance card of suitors growing full.

Then, it is gone, all gone, the way it used to be all gone when Jack's father was around. The fame dries up. Girls stay away. People start to look at Jack the way they did before. His mother is home every night now instead of out on the town, berating Jack for eating her food, using her tub, breathing too loud, taking up space, her nags and shouts worse than ever. When he closes his eyes at night, he hears her voice crackling in his head, then the ogress's roars, and he can no longer tell which is which.

Outside in the garden, the calf bleats with hunger. Jack lies against it, cuddling and soothing the babe until it falls asleep, the same way he did with poor old Milky White. But Jack can't sleep, thinking of how his calf will grow up like Milky, doomed to be sold, leaving Jack all alone, and it is just another reminder of how much he misses his dad. That's why he's been looking for a lass. To find a substitute for love. To have someone who cares. If Jack had all the riches in the world, he wouldn't buy clothes and jewels and houses like his mother did. He'd buy a new family. How much does it cost to buy that?

Lying in dead weeds, he gazes up at the bean-stalk, so green it fights the night, dwarfing all the stars. He doesn't dare go back up. That vile giantess would smite him dead. Nor can he show his face to that man again, who took care of him like a dad, before Jack stole from him like a common thief. But he had to. Because Jack's real dad *didn't* take care of him. That's the truth, he thinks, tears wetting his cheeks. His dad wasn't a hero. His dad left him to fend for himself. He promised Jack castles in the sky and never even got close. But Jack got close. So close. That's why he went up the beanstalk in the first place. To find a life bigger than the one his mother casts for him. And for a small, shining moment, he had. He'd been Jack the Great. Jack, who'd redeemed himself and his father both. If only he could go back up and try again . . . another bag of gold, or even two . . . maybe he could make a new life . . .

But gold runs out, just like it did before. Jack drops his eyes to the ground. There's no escape from his lot. His dad learned that lesson. Jack should chop that beanstalk, forget he ever had any magic beans. Otherwise, he'll end up in a ditch like his father, felled by his dreams. There's an ax against the garden fence. A few good wallops and it will all come down. . . .

But more days pass, and the beanstalk remains.

Then one night, his mother sneaks into the garden while he's sleeping, tries to steal the calf from under him. But the calf shrieks and wakes Jack just in time. His mother runs off, in no mood for a fight, but now Jack knows what she truly is, willing to sell his calf for high-priced veal, his precious calf that he risked his life for, before it even has a chance to grow. Ogres in the sky, ogres on the ground. There is no safe place for him anymore.

At dawn, he climbs the beanstalk.

When he reaches the top, the man is there.

Knew you'd come, he says.

He makes no mention of the gold, no mention of the calf. Instead, he leads Jack to the house, reminding him that the missus is out on her hunt, and they best be quick about things.

Breakfast is a banquet of wild-berry French toast, caramel cinnamon rolls, and candied apples.

Wasn't there a wicked witch who lured children to her house with sweet things so she could eat them? Jack says, mouth full.

It's too much work cookin' children, the man sighs.

Jack gulps. You've done it before?

I cook whatever the missus brings me. And plenty of kids like you come climbing for a new life.

Why are you helping me, then? Jack asks.

The man looks sad. I know what it's like. To want a new life. Difference is you're willing to try.

A stomping in the garden—

Jack's thrown from his chair, plates shatter, roars come blowing against the house.

Fee fi fo fum,
I smell the blood of a little one!

Into the oven goes Jack; the man sweeps up the mess—

The door bashes open, and she's there.

Mother Terror, hair wild, teeth bared, a dead peacock in each fist.

Where is he! Where is that good-for-nothing thief! He stole my calf! He stole my gold! I smell him in my house! Dirty, worthless thing! Bring him here, Husband! I'll grind his bones to make my bread!

Her husband waves her off. Don't be silly. No one stole anything. Calf ran off and you miscounted your gold. That's your feet you smell, need a good scrub.

Only thing that needs scrubbing is this house! his wife shouts. Lazy bag of bones, that's what you are! She dumps the peacocks on the table. Make yourself useful and cook these up! And bring me my golden harp! Better than hearing your yapping voice!

Jack watches the man bring forth a small, shimmering harp, made of gold, which the ogress clasps with stubby fingers, cueing the harp to play while it sheds golden flakes from its strings.

In time, the giant falls asleep.

Skit skat, the man frees Jack from the oven, pushes him on his way.

But when the man turns his back, Jack can't help himself. He snatches the harp, flees for the door—

The harp is magic though.

And magic things aren't taken lightly.

It lets out a cry: Master! Master!

The ogress jolts to life, eyes wide, nostrils flaring. In one lunge, she pounces for Jack, fists out to smash him—

A cauldron bludgeons her head, hurled from below. The giantess recoils, gaping at her husband, who throws another pot, then a dead peacock, then two. By the time his wife finds her senses, the man hoists Jack out the door, towards the beanstalk, the ogress chasing them both, hurling trees and stones in their path, her stomps punching craters in the sky.

The man hugs Jack to his breast.

You're doing this for me? Jack gasps.

Not for you, the man says. Because of you.

And now Jack understands.

One came up so the other could go down.

Both in search of a better life.

Together, they descend, the giantess leaping on the beanstalk, lumbering after them. But Jack is nimbler, shepherding the man down, in sight of the ground, before Jack breaks free and hops off first, calling for the man to follow him, but he's snared in vines, straight in the giant's sights.

Jack's mother rushes from the house, spotting the giant—

What have you done! she berates Jack. Idiot! Fool!

Jack grabs the ax.

He hacks at the beanstalk, chop, chop, chop, his mother cursing him from behind, the ogress cursing him from above—Dirty boy! Stupid boy! Worthless boy!—the sounds of their curses making him swing harder, harder, harder, until the space between sky and ground shrinks, ogress and mother about to meet, the giant's husband caught between.

Jump! Jack calls, holding arms out like a father to a son, and the man does, catching Jack like Jack catches him, the monsters screaming for them, closer, closer, before man and boy take the ax and swing it together, one, two, three—

The beanstalk falls, the giantess with it, a single clap of thunder that cleaves open the ground, both swallowed inside. A great cloud follows, dust pouring forth into sky, twinkling green in the sun, like little tiny seeds.

When it settles, Jack looks for his mother.

But she is nowhere to be found, as if she too has been sealed into the earth.

❦

Morning wakes Jack with a gentle kiss.

He snuggles into a furry belly and rolls over to hug the calf, already bigger than the day before.

He smells pancakes and sugar, the man whistling from the house.

Soon they'll have breakfast together and listen to the harp play lively songs, the harp the man hid in his coat when they fled, the harp that has long called the man its master. They'll watch gold flakes shed off gossamer strings, a good enough mound to buy them whatever they wish, but they'll just let it breeze and dance into the air like Christmas tinsel.

Then Jack will go into town and work hard at the mill, grinding grain into flour to make his bread. When he gets home, the man will give him a hug and kiss him good night before Jack bundles outside and sleeps with his calf, hugging and kissing her like the man kissed him, one family lost and another one found.

Never change, he whispers to his babe as he holds her, so clean and pure, wishing she would stay young like this forever.

But one day soon, he'll wake to a sweet stream of milk, and he'll realize that she's grown up, just like he has, against all odds, like a bean that sprouts into the sky, a bean people call magic, when the only magic it needed was love.

HANSEL
AND
GRETEL

NO ONE WANTS TO HEAR A TALE OF
warning.

And yet, children are told them all the time.

Stories about young boys and girls who stray
from the path and are punished for it.

But sometimes children have to find their own
way.

When the house turns from a sweet haven into
a cold witch's den.

When it's Mother or Father that's the witch.

Then deep into forbidden woods the children go.

Looking for the love they've lost.

Looking for a new place to call home.

Take the case of Hansel and Gretel.

Last you heard, it's about two fair-haired babes
who went off the forest path and nibbled a candy

house and nearly got baked into a pie for it. It's not surprising you heard that version, full of warnings that grumpy adults love. How else can a spirit like yours be kept tame and under control?

But that's not the true story of Hansel and Gretel.

Would you like to hear it?

The truth is full of warnings too.

But not for children.

Not for the children at all.

Once upon a time, in a village called Bagha Purana, two children lived in a house that smelled like sweets.

Everyone knew the house, because it was the house of Shakuntala, the best baker in the village, and her two children were the luckiest in the world because they got to try all her new delicacies before they were sold at the shop.

Rishi and Laxmi were their names, a boy and girl with brown, rosy cheeks and sunny dispositions. Laxmi was the precise planner, and Rishi

the bold thinker, which meant that together, they
could help Shakuntala tweak her recipes when a
ladoo or *jalebi* wasn't just right.

Needs a teensy bit more flavor, Laxmi might say.

What about rosewater? Rishi would propose.

Or saffron? Laxmi would chime.

Can't know until we try! Shakuntala then
piped, because unlike most parents in the village,
she trusted her children's instincts more than
her own.

During the day, Rishi and Laxmi would go
to school, and at night they would hang on their
mother like baby monkeys, pawing at her
black mane of hair and hefty bosom, while
she baked *burfi* and *rasmalai* and *gulab
jamun* and her famous *balu shah*, doting

on each piece until her husband, Atur, came home to taste them and rub his belly and moan *arehhhh*, and the challenge was to get him to moan it more than once. The next day, the fruits of Shakuntala's labor would be sold in his shop, Atur's Sweets, where he would take all the credit, because in those days women weren't allowed to be better than men, and Shakuntala was a better baker than any man, her husband included.

Naturally, everyone knew Shakuntala was making Atur's wares, but this was expected, wives slaving for their husbands out of sight while the husbands collected the earnings and acted the breadwinner of the house. But year after year, Shakuntala's sweets were so much better that no one in Bagha Purana wanted anything else, especially the children, who lined outside her shop for rosewater *ladoos* that would all be eaten by noon. Soon, kids stopped visiting the other bakeries in town, and one by one, they began to close. The men tried to compete, of course—offering discounts and free samples, scouring other towns for recipes to steal—but no one could touch Shakuntala, for she had the secret ingredients of love and humility and kindness, her baking only a means to bond with her Rishi and Laxmi, and who could compete with that? So the men of Bagha Purana did what men do when they're well beaten by a woman and can't find a way to fight fair. They pointed their fingers at her and screamed, *Witch!*

A trial is set.

What are the charges? Shakuntala asks.

Luring children with magical sweets, they say.

Witnesses are called.

Rishi and Laxmi defend their mother, and for a moment the outcome is in doubt. Perhaps if their father defended his wife too, then she would have escaped unscathed. But he is ashamed that people are saying out loud that the sweets in his shop aren't his, even if it's the truth. He wonders if he could bake even better sweets than his wife without her around. So he stays quiet. This seals Shakuntala's fate.

Once a wife and mother, now a witch.

The men put out her eyes and lose her deep in the forest, so she will never find her way back.

Rishi and Laxmi go looking for her, night after night, year after year, but it is no use.

She is gone.

In time, the father marries again.

Her name is Divya Simla. She's much younger than Atur and wears short dresses that show off her bony legs, and she looks like she's never eaten a sweet in her life. But she pretends to be a good baker and to love his children, long enough to be his bride, then gives up the pretense entirely. Soon Rishi and Laxmi realize that their father has married a witch, a *real* witch, who despises children and only cares about herself.

There is nothing scarier to a child than a mother who hates being one.

Bad luck hits the house. The bakery fails, the children catch a chill, the toilets overflow. The house is always cold, even on sweltering days, and smells sour and stale, nothing like it used to. Whatever money Atur has stored is spent on doctors for Rishi and Laxmi and trying to keep them fed. All the while, Divya Simla stews, her eyes screwing into the children like two tiny curses.

One night, after they're supposed to be asleep, Rishi and Laxmi overhear Divya Simla whispering to their father.

Don't you see? They're causing all our bad luck!

They've ruined our lives, grubbing up all our money and food. And for what! What do they give us in return other than sour looks that I am not their mother! We need to get rid of them!

Atur protests: Get rid of my own children?

If we don't, we will all die, says Divya Simla. Bad luck only gets worse.

The next day, lightning strikes the house and burns half of it to the ground.

That night, Rishi and Laxmi hear Divya Simla and their father.

I can't take any more bad luck, Atur pleads.

Then you know what we have to do, Divya Simla insists.

Atur despairs. But . . . but . . .

I'll take them into the forest and leave them there, Divya Simla resolves. They are children. They'll be fine. One day they will grow up and thank us for teaching them to stand on their own two feet.

Atur says nothing.

Rishi and Laxmi know what it means when their father says nothing. Just like he'd said nothing when it came time to protect their mother.

What to do, Laxmi? Rishi frets.

Leave it to me, says his sister.

The next morning, Divya Simla kicks them with a bony foot.

Get up! Get up! Time to go!

Where? Laxmi asks.

To chop some wood to fix the house, says Divya Simla.

But Rishi and Laxmi notice that their step-mother brings no ax.

Laxmi is prepared though. She scoops ash from the burnt parts of the house into her pockets, and as she and her brother are led deep into the forest, Laxmi lags behind, sprinkling the cinders on the ground to chart their path.

Good thinking, sister, Rishi whispers.

What are you two doing! Divya Simla shouts, peeking back suspiciously.

Rishi had to do pee-pee, Laxmi calls.

Stop dawdling! Divya Simla barks.

Still, brother and sister take their time, making sure they're out of view as Laxmi drops her little ashes.

Now what are you doing! Divya Simla growls.

Laxmi's turn to do pee-pee, says Rishi.

But there is a limit to how much pee-pee can be

done, and eventually they are so far into the forest
that the sun no longer shines through and the trees
are dark and crooked.

Stay there. I'll come back for you, says Divya
Simla, hustling away.

Hours pass. Laxmi and Rishi play a game of
pickup sticks and dance to made-up songs—*What
is worse than rain all day? What is worse than a dog
who won't play? Divya Simla, Divya Simla!*—before
they've had their fun and follow the ashes all the
way home.

When they knock on the door, their father
answers and falls to his knees with happiness.

Behind him, Divya Simla's face hardens to a
lump of coal.

There you are! What took you so long? she
snaps.

Divya Simla isn't to be trusted, but she did prove
right on one account.

Bad luck only gets worse.

A few weeks later, a drought falls upon the

village, killing all the vegetables and starving the animals. No one has anything to eat. What little bread Atur can forage from his friends and neighbors isn't enough to feed him and his wife and his children.

At night, the whispering begins again.

You have to choose between me and them, Divya Simla tells Atur. We don't have enough for both.

God sent them back to us, Atur protests. They

are my flesh and blood.

And what am I? I married you when no one else would and now you'd let me die? Divya Simla hounds. They are old enough to take care of themselves. They're not our responsibility. And besides: bad luck only gets worse.

How could our luck get any worse? asks Atur.

Keep them here and see, Divya Simla warns.

Atur says nothing.

In their bed, Laxmi hugs Rishi tight.

What we will do, brother? she asks.

Leave it to me, Rishi answers.

The next day, Divya Simla takes her stepchildren to the forest, this time to hunt for wild berries, even though she brings no basket and any berries are long dead by the drought. Their father can't even look at them as they go.

But Rishi has a plan. At breakfast, he pretended to eat his dry, stale *chapati* and instead slipped it in his pocket. Now as they walk deeper into the woods, he sprinkles the crumbs behind him.

Good thinking, Laxmi whispers.

What are you doing back there! Divya Simla puffs.

Looking for flowers for you! Rishi pips.

Divya Simla scowls. I don't like flowers! Don't waste time!

Yes, Stepmother, says Laxmi.

All the while, Rishi scatters his bread crumbs.

Divya Simla takes them so far into the forest that Rishi and Laxmi can't even see their own shadows anymore. Crows shriek with warning: this is no place for children.

Stay there. I'll come back for you, says Divya Simla, scuttling away.

This time, Rishi and Laxmi are too scared to play games or sing songs. Slitted eyes blink at them between trees. Rustles echo from the underbrush. Cold, slithering things brush their ankles and necks. They clutch each other and count to one hundred, then follow the bread crumbs back—

But they're gone.

All eaten up by the crows that now mock them in piercing caws, as if to say: *Divya Simla, Divya Simla, Divya Simla!*

There is no path home.

Laxmi points east: It's this way.

Rishi points west: No, it's this way.

Laxmi is more stubborn. East they go. They walk the entire night and the next day, from morning until evening, but it's clear that they're nowhere close to Bagha Purana, let alone their father's house. They're starving now, more than children can bear, and their legs are too weak to carry them. Holding hands, they crumble beneath a bush and sink into sleep. Neither is sure they'll wake up. But somehow they do, one by one, with just enough life to pry open their eyes.

Two crows glare back.

The first drops something in front of Rishi.

A frosted pink sweet.

He swallows it.

Mmm, rosewater, he says. My favorite!

The second crow drops a yellow sweet in front of Laxmi, who stuffs it in her mouth.

Saffron, she says. My favorite!

The crows flutter ahead, and brother and sister follow, still tasting heaven in their mouths.

A short while later, they come to a little house. The crows land on the doorstep, and when the kids inch closer, they see the house is made from pistachio-cardamom bread with a roof of milky-fudge balls and windows glassed in clear, sticky honey.

Brother and sister glance at each other, like two desert wanderers witnessing a mirage.

Is it real? Laxmi asks.

Rishi peeks in the honey-glass and breathes in the crisp, fresh smell. He breaks off a tiny piece and pops it in his mouth.

We can't eat a stranger's house! Laxmi scolds. What would Mama say?

She would say be smart and stay alive, Rishi answers. I can't see anyone through the window. Quick, quick, before they get home!

He's already climbing onto the creamy roof, while Laxmi raids the doughy walls, each stuffing their face with green and white sweets, their bellies swelling, their minds numb with sugar, before a gentle voice floats from inside:

Nibble, nibble, little mouse,
Who is eating at my house?

The door opens, and crows fly out like bats from a cave, and with them, a woman, like they've given birth to her, her brawny body wrapped in black billowing robes, a tall black hat on her head, a black veil over her face, a lumpy cane in her fist.

Daring thing to eat a witch's house, she taunts, lurching toward them. Wonder what kind of a mother raised *you*. . . .

Rishi and Laxmi start to flee, but crows surround them, talons hooking their shoulders, flying the two children toward the house, toward the witch. She grabs them in her big, meaty hands, inhaling their skin like flesh for her ovens. Brother and sister let out twin, tortured screams—

Rishi? Laxmi?

Her voice is a soft hiss.

She pulls back her veil.

Mama? the children gasp.

Shakuntala hugs them to her breast and doesn't let go. I can't see you, but I know my babies, my beautiful, perfect babies.

The children drink in her scent of sugar and spice and begin to cry.

All these years I waited, my crows searching for any children wandering the woods, she says. Those fools in Bagha Purana accused me of luring children with sweets. Well, that's how I've gone and found you, haven't I—

She feels their bony limbs and waists.

Why are you like skeletons? What's happened? Where's your father?

In Bagha Purana, Laxmi says.

With Divya Simla, Rishi says.

Shakuntala frowns.

Come inside and tell Mama everything.

When their tale of woe is finished, even the crows feel sorry for them.

Shakuntala taps her fingers on the table, her blinded eyes fixed on the children, as if she's watching them.

Rishi and Laxmi peer around the house, stacked with sweets of every color in crooked towers from floor to ceiling, familiar ones like *gulab jamuns* and *ladoos*, along with new inventions, *rasgullas, khalakand, nankhatais,* shedding brilliant sugardust all around, like they're in a fairy's cave. An oven baking gold-leaf cakes spits embers of fire and gilded puffs. Meanwhile, black crows glare down from every corner like sentinels.

Shakuntala speaks. When I was alone in the

forest, these birds saved me, bringing me bits of berries and food. Must have sensed a kindred spirit. Crows are outcasts of the forest, just like me. In return, I feed them and keep them safe from hawks and foxes as if they are my children. And I told them about my Rishi and Laxmi and the shape of their faces and the sound of their voices and how they must be out there in the woods, looking for me . . .

We did look for you, Mama, says Rishi.

I know you did, says Shakuntala. But happy endings are not won so easily. Justice takes time. And it sounds like there is still some justice to be done.

She taps her fingers on the table in the same rhythm the crows cawed in the woods, as if she's thinking, *Divya Simla, Divya Simla, Divya Simla.* All around, her birds seem to smile as if they sense mischief at work.

Tell me, says Shakuntala. How far is Bagha Purana from here?

We don't know! The crows ate all the crumbs! says Rishi.

They erased the path we made! Laxmi echoes.

Shakuntala leans in. Did they, now? Naughty things. That's how they found you, I'm sure. Nibbling after you, bit by bit, from wherever you came . . .

She lifts her head toward her crows, matching their grins. Which means they also know the way *back*.

In Bagha Purana, souls pray to the goddess Durga.

No rain has fallen for two hundred and twenty days, and the plague continues unabated.

In Atur's house, the mood is dark. The husband has lost his children and is left with a wife whose harebrained schemes to make money are as rotten as they are futile.

What if we pay a *pundit* to tell the people that you are Durga's favorite son and they must all give us money to appease the gods? Divya Simla says excitedly. Or what if we put dirt in little cups and sell them to the village for five rupees and say if they plant their crops with it, then they will sprout without water?

And what happens when they don't sprout? Atur asks.

We will blame them for not doing proper blessings, Divya Simla huffs.

Atur says nothing.

Then one day, he hears the cry of crows outside his door, harsh and relentless like an alarm. He opens his door, and there is a box on the ground. Lifting the lid, he finds twelve beautiful pastel colored *mitai*, rich with milk and honey and fruit, none of which thrive in Bagha Purana anymore.

Atur tastes one and his heart stirs, a riot of sugar and love and magic on his tongue, a reminder of the

way his wife's baking once made him feel. Shakun-tala is long dead, of course, or at least he keeps her that way in his heart. Which means sweets like these can only have been sent by God, a gift to tide Atur over until better luck comes.

His wife's voice cracks like a whip behind him. What are those? Where did they come from?

She tastes one, and her eyes go big.

We can sell them in the village, Atur offers. A few rupees each. It'll give us enough to get by until the drought is done.

But Divya Simla isn't looking at him. She's peering through the door at the ground strewn with pastel-colored crumbs in a neat little trail toward the forest.

There's more where those came from, she says, with a toothy grin. Stay here. By the time I'm back, we'll have enough sweets to open a new bakery, ten rupees a taste!

Atur tries to argue that they shouldn't tempt fate that's finally been kind to them, but his wife is tramping into the woods, and as she fades through the trees, Atur feels a light mist from above, as if the clouds are remembering how to rain.

In time, Divya Simla comes to the house

made of bread and sweets. She kicks her heels in the air and does a twirl, convinced her luck is changed, now that she's rid of those awful children. With both fists, she punches holes in the pistachio-cardamom walls, stuffing her pockets with as much as she can take, then climbs the roof and jams balls of milky fudge into the back of her dress, padding her bony backside.

There's enough here for ten bakeries! she thinks. Better rush home and fetch some baskets.

She turns on her heel, back into the woods—

A voice sings on the wind.

Nibble, nibble, little mouse,
Who is eating at my house?

The door to the house opens, and Divya Simla stops cold, arms full of bread.

Witch! she gasps.

The woman in black gazes back at her, with scarred eyes and crows perched on her shoulders.

And yet *you're* the one eating *my* house, the witch speaks.

There is a plague in my village! Divya Simla cries. I was taking just enough to sell so me and my poor children can stay alive!

Ah, your children . . . , says the witch. How many?

Two! pipes Divya Simla.

And their names?

Rishi and Laxmi! Please, Divya Simla begs. Please let me get home to them.

The witch purses her lips. The crows on her shoulders glance at each other.

I would never deprive a mother of her children, nor children of a mother. It is an unforgivable crime, the witch says. If you speak the truth, then you must hurry back.

Thank you, Divya Simla breathes with relief, shuffling away—

But what will happen when you run out of what you've taken? the witch asks. I can always bake more sweets, but you have hardly enough to sell.

Crows swoop and snatch bread out of Divya Simla's hands, making a meal of it.

And now you have even less, the witch sighs. Naughty things. Come inside, my dear. I'll give you my recipes and some ingredients to carry with you, so you and your children will thrive.

Your recipes? Divya Simla says, her eyes gleaming before they turn wary. And in return?

In return, you keep a lonely old woman company and tell me all about your Rishi and Laxmi, says the witch. A fair trade, don't you think?

Divya Simla grins.

Finally, those two children would be of use.

A fair trade, indeed.

Inside the house, Divya Simla doesn't see the wonder of the colorful sweets freshly baked and the shimmer of sugardust in the air and the steamy scent of honeymilk.

She only sees money. A trove of treasure just for her. Starving people in Bagha Purana will pay any price for such sweets, and she won't offer a single discount.

How much can I take? Divya Simla asks the witch, her eyes pinned on the shelves of flour, eggs, and jars of whipping cream, along with sheets of loose paper, scrawled with a baker's notes.

And what recipes will you give me? Divya Simla

hounds. I need your best ones if my children are to survive.

Take anything you wish, the witch offers without hesitation. Only thing I can't give you is my recipe for *shakuntala*, of course. That is too precious.

Divya Simla's eyes glimmer. *Shakuntala?*

It is a sweet baked with so much love that it is too priceless to be sold, says the witch. A single taste of it and a person can never get enough. They will pay any price for more: their horse, their jewels, their house . . . anything you ask.

From inside a silver tiffin, she draws a heart-shaped sweet the color of blood, sprinkled with golden crystals of sugar.

None but the bravest souls would even be willing to try, the witch winks.

Divya Simla is so entranced she can only give a little squeak.

The witch holds it up, and Divya Simla takes it into her mouth. Coconut, chocolate, and buttery rose shiver on her tongue and slide down her throat, making her body tingle all over. Atur's sweets tasted dull and impotent. But this . . . this is alchemy, like the nectar of Durga herself. She would sell her soul for another bite, just as the witch warned. And if she is willing to sell such things for it, imagine what others would pay!

I must have the recipe, Divya Simla demands. I cannot leave without the secrets of *shakuntala!*

All around, the crows screech and snicker.

The witch seems to quell a smile. I'm afraid that is not possible.

Divya Simla's face twists. You would deprive a mother of saving her children?

For the first time, the witch loses her poise. There is a hardness to her jaw, a fire heating up her skin. But then it is gone as quickly as it came.

Forgive me, I am being too stubborn, she says. I, too, was once a mother. I know what real love is and the lengths a mother will go to save her young. But the recipe isn't one that can be written down. It must be experienced, secrets and all. Shall we make some together, then?

Yes! Yes! Divya Simla touts. Enough to feed all of Bagha Purana!

The witch is already pushing her to the shelves, calling out ingredients—cocoa! rosewater! butter-cream! eggs! cardamom! cinnamon!—as the crows retrieve and drop them into Divya Simla's arms and she brings them all to the pot, spilling them in, as the witch waves her arm like a wand, singsonging her instructions. Beat the eggs, then pour the cream, then cocoa, then rose, then a pinch of the rest, before you blow kisses into the mix, thinking of those you love. . . .

Divya Simla blows kisses, thinking only of herself.

The witch blows her own kisses before hoisting up the pot. And now, when it is ready, we take it to the oven and bake it with the secret ingredient that makes all the difference. . . .

Divya Simla chases behind. What's the secret ingredient? Tell me! Tell me!

Open the oven and find out for yourself, the witch chimes.

Divya Simla tugs the oven door and screams.

There are two children inside, a boy and girl, bound and gagged like pigs about to be roasted.

They gape back with soot-covered faces and scared eyes, like she's their savior come to rescue them.

Divya Simla is dead white, her voice a toad's croak.

Rishi?

Laxmi?

Behind her, the witch gives a belly laugh. These two? Your Rishi and Laxmi? Don't be ridiculous! I found them in the woods, starving and abandoned by their mother, and you just said your children are at *home*.

Y-y-yes, Divya Simla sputters. Of course—

Good, says the witch, because these two I fattened up nice and plump, since you can't make *shakuntala* without the secret ingredient and now you know what the secret is: *unloved children*. All you have to do is shove the pot in with them and their flavor will be baked right in. Then you'll have enough *shakuntala* to last a thousand days! Now go on. Go on!

Divya Simla clutches her throat. Bake children . . . ? But . . . but . . .

Oh, I see, the witch says, going cold. Take the other sweets, then.

She shuts the oven door—

Wait! Divya Simla says, her mind tossing and turning. She can't leave without this treasure. She can't sacrifice her *shakuntala*! And why should she?

Why should she care if those two brats are baked? They are not hers, after all. And it was they who cursed her house and Bagha Purana and put her and Atur in this mess. Getting rid of them wouldn't be cruelty—it would be an act of love for her fellow villagers, a triumph of Good over Evil! And there is no question these two children are Evil, simply by their very existence. No wonder they ended up in a witch's oven—bad luck follows them everywhere! Well, now, it is time to burn away this Evil once and for all.

Divya Simla opens the oven door and glares the children down. Put the batter in, she orders.

If the witch is surprised, she doesn't show it.

Not yet, she replies. First you must prime the oven and make sure it's warm.

Divya Simla hesitates. How do I do that?

Get in yourself, naturally, the witch says. Have you never baked before?

Oh, right, Divya Simla puffs.

She climbs her bony legs in, hunches beside the children in a tight little ball, and the witch closes the door.

The oven is ice-cold.

Brother and sister stare silently at her.

Divya Simla avoids their eyes.

Is it warm enough? the witch calls outside.

No! It's frigid! says Divya Simla impatiently.

Oh dear. Should have primed it before I added the children, the witch sighs. She opens the door and drags out the hog-tied siblings, then shuts it again, leaving Divya Simla inside. Let me try again. . . .

For a moment, Divya Simla is relieved to be rid of the children and their horrible stares.

Then she feels the heat.

Is it warm enough now? says the witch.

Yes, yes! Divya Simla snaps, the sweets stuffed in her dress starting to melt. She kicks at the oven door—

It stays shut.

She shoves her body against it.

Nope.

Locked.

Fire roars somewhere beneath.

What's happening! she shouts. What are you doing!

Two young voices answer from outside.

Stay there, says a boy.

We'll come back for you, says the girl.

And all the crows laugh.

Rishi and Laxmi slide a sticky black pudding out of the oven and taste it with their thumbs. These days, they are round in the belly and ruddy in the cheeks, hugging close to their mother's side. Rain lashes the roof, wind howls in the trees, and a mongoose gapes glowing eyes through the window, but inside there is warmth and laughter and spice, all the ingredients for a home. Soon, no one remembers any home before this one, as if love sweeps away bad memories, like birds eating up crumbs in a forest. Brother and sister take one more bite and peer at each other.

Needs cinnamon, says Rishi.

Just a pinch, says Laxmi.

Can't know until we try! Shakuntala pipes, gliding to the shelf.

Laxmi looks around the quiet house, not a stir in the corners. Mama, where do all the crows go at night?

Why do they fly away and come back at

dawn? Rishi echoes.

Shakuntala smiles. Must be their secret, she says.

But she knows, of course.

That each night, after her baking is done and the children sent to bed, the crows fly off to Bagha Purana and leave three sweets on her husband's doorstep, the very best of the batch. There he'll find them in the morning and taste the love his house was once made of, moaning *arehhhhhh*, once, twice, thrice, before silence comes and a bright, vacant sun and he remembers all that's been lost.

IMAGINE A BOY SO BEAUTIFUL HE
drains the light from all those around him.

He is incandescent, with smooth brown skin
that blushes like a rose, tight curls of black hair,
a strong, dimpled jaw, and a wide, teasing mouth.
He looks like a cupid—but of the earth, not the
sky—a childish spirit packed into a powerful, mus-
cular frame. He charms every girl who meets him,
most boys too, and none leave his presence without
thinking about him endlessly, as if he's hexed them,
turning hearts to stone for any but him.

He is also the youngest prince of a famed kingdom, with three brothers before him, the older
princes still unmarried because any suitable girl
wants the youngest, even if she must wait for him,
even if he comes at the cost of a crown.

The king and queen grow alarmed. Beauty is a

gift, but not when it means sacrificing three good sons who should sire heirs!

So they send him away, their most beautiful boy, because everyone in the palace will shine a little bit brighter without him. Or so they think. Get too used to glorious sunsets and it is easy to blame the sun for stealing the clouds' glory—but withhold the sun and there is nothing to see.

Too late, he is gone now, banished into the woods, where the first creature he comes across is a hunched old fairy who brings him to her fairyland high up in the trees and dotes on him like a mother. At last someone cares about who he is on the inside, who makes him feel safe, and he asks her questions about love and how to find it so he can love someone the way everyone thinks they love him. The old fairy just smiles. Every night, there is a freshly made bed in a colorful treehouse and a banquet of sunflower greens, root vegetable pie, and buttercream cake. All the other fairies in the kingdom sneak one peek at the prince and want to marry him, which means the prince doesn't have a moment's peace, but the elder fairy swoops in and beats them off. The prince is thankful for her protection until

one day, the old fairy traps
him in a tree and declares her
love, the love she's been hiding all
this time, then demands he kiss her
and make her his bride. When the prince
refuses, she flies into a rage and tells him that
from now on, he will live as a beast so no one shall
ever behold his beauty again, not until he receives
true love's kiss, the kiss he should have had with
her. She spits a black, smoky spell and pushes him
from the trees into the cold lake below.

The prince feels relieved, honestly.

He is ordinary now. Maybe he can find real love.

But then he sees himself in the lake's mirror and
realizes that, as there is beauty, there is ugliness
too, the kind of ugliness which drives people away

just as beauty once brought them too close. Both faces cloud out hope for love.

He will be alone forever.

Far away, in a town called Mont de Marsan, a rich merchant named Lieu Wei has three sons and three daughters.

They are the only family of their kind in this land, the father having crossed an ocean to sell his wares here, again, again, again, until he saw opportunity in living among his customers. His three sons help with the business, so they're always on a ship going here and there, while the two older daughters strut about town and flaunt their sumptuous furs and gems on pale, thin fingers and search for men to marry them. This is a challenge because Lieu Wei's daughters are used to the finest things and need to marry rich men. But men are either handsome or rich, and those who are both tend to be criminals. So the daughters hunt the handsome ones, but handsome men don't want women of their kind, not unless they're rich, and the merchants' daughters aren't quite the richest. Thus, the daughters berate their father to make more and more money, for how else can they be wed?

The youngest daughter, meanwhile, stays at home. She has no interest in marriage or diamonds and spends her days reading books and tending to her father, keeping him well-fed and his house spotlessly clean, her latest book tucked in the back pocket of her apron as she brings a pot to boil.

I gave you the name Mei, which means *beauty*, and yet here you are clinging to your father and acting like a maid, Lieu Wei chuckles. You can't marry your books. How will you find a man to take care of you?

One spoiled man in my life is enough, Mei winks.

How can I be spoiled when I tell you to go? her father asks.

Would you be as happy without me here? Mei replies.

No, sighs Lieu Wei.

Mei brings him his favorite pearl tea and corn crab soup.

When this next shipment is sold, I will be the

richest man in Mont de Marsan, says Lieu Wei.
Then all three of you will be married and I'll make
sure the best man goes to you.

Mei smiles. I hope he is good in the kitchen,
because I'll be right here with you.

Lieu Wei shakes his head. So much beauty
wasted on a girl whose heart is her true virtue.

But Mei isn't doting on her father out of virtue.
She finds him stubborn, arrogant, and obsessed
with money. Yet playing the dutiful daughter has
benefits. She can stay at home and read her books,
while her sisters hunt for husbands. Men in this
town are boorish and bigoted. They look at you
instead of *see* you. Mei wants nothing to do with
them, let alone tie herself to one for life. Even so,
men have the money in this world and they wield it
over women to turn them into brides. An unmarried woman here might as well be a beast. So she
sticks close to her father, and whenever he gives gold
to her sisters for new dresses and boots, he also slips
her some, which Mei uses to buy new books, while
the rest she buries under a floorboard so she can
one day live free of men entirely in a house of her
own with a library two stories high and a garden

where she can read. A few more years of duty and sacrifice and her dream will be secure . . .

Then the ship sinks.

The ship with her father's new wares, the one he bet his riches upon to make himself richer.

Mei's dreams fall to the bottom of the sea.

Lieu Wei is poor now, so poor that his three sons find jobs with his rivals and his eldest daughters cry in their rooms all day. Even Lieu Wei can hardly get out of bed, loafing about in his pajamas, demanding pearl tea and corn crab soup, even though there is no money to afford them. But Mei won't give up. She wants her house, she wants her library and garden, so she writes letters to bankers in towns near and far who might be willing to invest in her father. When no response comes, Mei persists, reminding them that Lieu Wei was once the richest man in Mont de Marsan and will be again.

At last a single reply—a banker in faraway Toulouse—willing to meet Mei's father and see if a deal can be worked out.

Mei stuffs Lieu Wei into his best suit, saddles his underfed horse. Her older sisters peek out of their rooms.

Toulouse? They're famous for handbags, says the first. Buy me one, Father!

They have nice hats too! I want one! says the second.

Now that our troubles are solved, I'll bring you two of each! Lieu Wei crows, before turning to Mei, with love in his eyes, for it was his youngest and fairest who made this all possible. And what would you like, Mei?

Mei wants only for him to impress the banker, to close the deal, so that she and her father can go back to their old arrangement—she takes care of him, so that one day, when his life runs out, hers can begin. But she cannot say this, nor does she want the silly gifts her sisters want, so instead she thinks of the house she'll have and the thousand books and the flowers in the garden in which she'll read them and says:

If you see a rose, Father . . .

He kisses her on the cheek. The best rose from here to Toulouse, he vows.

Lieu Wei rides to Toulouse, but the meeting

does not go well. He is so used to being rich and people courting his favor that now that his fortunes have reversed, he has forgotten how to be humble. He makes the banker feel small, and no one wants to invest in someone like that. Plenty of other fish in the sea. So Lieu Wei is sent off empty-handed and he rides back home, silently cursing the banker, for he is incapable of blaming himself.

But slowly his mood lifts. He has only thirty miles left, a light snow falling, and he knows that even though there is no deal to celebrate or hand-bags or hats for his daughters, Mei will greet him with a smile and a kiss, and he thinks about how lucky he is to have a daughter who loves him uncon-ditionally. He must be sure to find her a prime husband when the time comes; he can't bear the thought of her all alone into old age, reading books in quiet rooms. It is because of these thoughts that he takes his focus off the path and finds himself at the edge of an unfamiliar forest. The snow turns into a storm, the gale so heavy it blinds his view. Into the forest he rides, but night adds an extra veil, blacking out the trees, the snow relentless, monotonous in every direction, and now he's going in circles, sure that he'll die of hunger or the cold or the wolves that he hears howling lustily on the wind. In a daze, he shouts Mei's name, like a magical word that can save him, before he's blown off his horse, into a grave of white—

Then a bright light glows, deep in the trees.

Limping toward it, he finds an enormous castle at the end of a grove, all the windows golden with flame. The gates are open, the path well lit. Lieu Wei leaves his horse in a small, warm barn where there is a bucket of fresh apples. Then he raps the knocker on the front door, and when no one answers, he finds the door unlocked and lets himself in. A fire burns in the great hall, and near it a long table sparkles with silver dishes filled with sumptuous food: a potage of beef with horseradish cream, field mushrooms with cheese, haunches of roast venison with marmalade, slow-roast pork belly and sage apples, buttered cauliflower, parsnip mash, and plum-and-thyme custard tarts. But there is only one place setting. Lieu Wei is so famished and so used to Mei serving him that he doesn't think twice about taking his place in the chair and eating until his belly hurts. He knows he should ride straight home, but he can hardly move in this state, so he creeps through the castle, just to see what's around, envious of its solarium and library and gardens, before he finds a firelit room with the door open, the bed turned down with goose-feather blankets and fluffed-up pillows, and he can't help but tuck himself in, because this is the way Mei makes his bed at home.

When he opens his eyes, it is morning. A pile of clean clothes in his size lie next to him, along with a velvet box holding two gem-crusted combs, which Lieu Wei packs into his coat, thinking them perfect gifts for his daughters. There is also a tray of eggs and buttered toast and a mug of hot chocolate. A more modest man would ask who is providing these things and why, but Lieu Wei thinks little of it, as if he's a guest at a luxurious hotel. After eating and dressing, he heads to the barn to fetch his horse, which is already waiting by the gate, rested and well-fed, beneath an arbor of roses.

He is about to ride off when he remembers Mei and what she asked for and glances up at the lush flowers over his head. He plucks the best one and smells its sweet folds before slipping it into his coat.

Then he hears a sound and sees something bounding out of the castle, a monstrous form with a swamp-colored face, hairy and horrible, and the horns of a devil. Lieu Wei topples from his horse in shock, scrambles back—

You are very ungrateful, the monster seethes. I saved your life by giving you shelter in my castle and you repay me by plucking my favorite roses. Let's see what happens when I pluck out your insides.

Lieu Wei clasps his hands: I'm sorry, my liege! Please spare me! I picked it for my daughter, who asked for only a rose out of all the gifts in the world—

Don't call me 'my liege.' Call me 'Beast,' because that is how you see me. Look at how you tremble. Look at how you cast your eyes away. Look at how badly you want to be free from me! the monster snarls, looming over him.

Then his horrible face becomes a little less horrible, as if he is thinking something over. Of all the gifts in the world, your daughter chose only a rose? he asks.

She is as humble and good as she is fair, Lieu Wei pleads. She is called Mei. Named for her beauty inside and out. Please. I must get home to her.

The Beast stiffens. His humped nose twitches. Fine, he growls. Go home.

Lieu Wei falls at his feet. Thank you, kind Beast—

But if you leave alive, then you are to send Mei to take your place by nightfall, the Beast demands. If you fail, then I shall find you and your family and tear all of you to pieces. Your choice. Die now or promise your daughter in your place.

Lieu Wei loses his breath. But . . . but . . .

The Beast roars in his face, and Lieu Wei is so scared he leaps on his horse and flees into the forest, sealing his promise.

He resolves not to tell Mei of what's happened— they'll move houses, they'll shift towns, they'll sail to the edge of the world to escape this ungodly demon. But what if he follows them? What if he finds them wherever they go?

He tries to put on a smile once he's home. His eldest daughters pose with their new combs in their hair, caring nothing about how it went in Toulouse and only how they look in the mirror. But Mei knows her father too well. When he gives her the rose, she sees his anguish as if this gift came at the steepest price, and she wheedles him until he confesses everything: the failed meeting, the snowstorm and castle and Beast who nearly killed him, and the promise the Beast demanded when he set Lieu Wei free.

Don't be scared, he says now, holding Mei's hand. I will never let that monster have you.

But Mei doesn't look scared at all. Her dark eyes twinkle as she leans forward.

Tell me about this Beast. Is he rich?

So rich that even the doorknobs are made of solid gold, says her father.

And the castle is big? Mei inquires.

Like a palace, with grand halls and a library and a garden and so many rooms I could hardly find my way out.

And there was no one else living there but the Beast? Mei asks.

Not even a mouse.

I see, Mei replies. Then I must go and take your place just as you said.

Lieu Wei blanches. Why?

Because you made a deal, says Mei.

Lieu Wei grabs her, trying to talk her out of it, but there is no use—he knows his daughter's resolve is as strong as her virtue.

But virtue has nothing to do with why Mei agrees to the Beast's terms.

Instead, she's thinking of another reason to go to the castle with a library and a garden and no one else living in it.

So she can kill the Beast.

No one would care, would they?

The castle would be hers.

It sounds like a nice place to grow old in.

The murder doesn't go as planned.

She is well prepared though. A dagger belted to her leg under her dress, the steel cold against her skin as she kicks her horse. The horse knows the way and rides untroubled, thinking another bucket of apples will be its reward. She makes sure to arrive at the Beast's castle with light still left, so she isn't ambushed in the dark. Through the gates, the horse canters, before she pulls it to a stop in front of the castle.

She's surprised at how unafraid she is.

Perhaps it's because she hates this Beast already.

Killing a daughter in her father's place?

Reveling in the torment of a young girl?

How predictable.

He might be a monster, but he is very much a man.

A snap of sticks—

She turns to find the Beast standing by the barn beneath the arbor of roses, holding a tray with chocolate hearts and two glasses of champagne. He is as her father described: a strange, brackish green, with wide-set yellow eyes and a pinched nose, like a mangled lion born at the bottom of the sea. But he does not roar, nor does he attack. He is wearing a freshly steamed suit, and he has curled and ribboned the fringes of his fur. Gaping at her, he shifts from one hairy foot to the other, unsure what happens next.

Mei realizes her father had it wrong.

This Beast has no intention of killing her.

He wants her company.

For Mei, that is worse than death.

You are my prisoner now, he bellows. You can never go home again. You will live here forever.

We'll see, she says, walking into his house.

The castle is so rich and beautiful that it doesn't

seem forged by humans. Statues smile down at her; the window curtains draw a little wider to light her path; a mirror even says, This way!, as if it knows what she is looking for. Because it is the library she cares about, and when she finds it, she drops to her knees, because it is higher than the highest house in Mont de Marsan and as vast as a royal ballroom, with magical ladders that bend to the floor and scoop her right up, whizzing her from romance on high to mysteries down low to fantasy in between, each shelf like an exotic land because men back home only hoarded books about shipwrecks and jungles, but here are so many books, too many books, and she doesn't know where to begin. That's when she notices the Beast peeking from the door, still holding his chocolate hearts, and she thinks this is the moment where she should kill him, so she can read in peace—

Try this one, he says.

He plucks a book from the lowest shelf and puts it on the table.

Then he's gone.

The mirrors point her to her room, which is out-landish in size and has three closets, filled to the brim with dresses and shoes she'd never wear, but the bed is comfortable and she curls up with pillows and gives the book a try. It is not about shipwrecks or jungles but about a man named Bluebeard who is so handsome and rich that he takes wife after wife, testing each one to obey his rules and cutting off their heads when they don't, until finally one girl escapes and a dark, handsome prince rescues her before he stabs Bluebeard in the heart. The End.

She snaps the book shut, loud enough to spook the mirrors in the hall, which whisper, My word! and Oh dear!, as if they've gotten too used to silence.

Dinner is served at six, and she picks a dress from the closet that is heavy and silver and looks like a suit of armor.

The table in the grand hall glistens with truffle lobster salad, pheasant confit, hen egg custard, chateaubriand, salted shortbread, and raspberry lemon curd—but Mei just asks for some broth and rice, which the Beast goes and fetches for her without delay, and she wonders who is doing the cooking.

The castle is enchanted by fairies, he says, reading her mind. They found me wandering in a forest and brought me here. Fairies have always liked me. They see beneath the surface. They see who you are.

A new wrinkle, Mei thinks. Will the fairies like *her*? She doesn't want to be an unwelcome guest in her own house. Perhaps she should wait to kill him until she gets these fairies on her side. A difficult task, given she can't even see them—

Did you enjoy the book? he asks.

She looks up. I didn't know Beasts read books.

When I read a book I'm not a Beast, he says. He asks again: Did you like the book?

Not particularly, she answers. A girl should fight her own battles against a monster. Not call in a prince.

He stares at her a long while.

I'll leave another one tomorrow, he says.

They eat in silence, his manners better than she expected. As she reads in the garden by twilight, she finds herself wondering what book he will give her. She's always chosen them for herself. But now she's thinking about what awaits: the length, the feel, the smell of it . . . When she undresses at night, she finds the dagger strapped to her leg and scarcely remembers what it is for. Better to leave it though. Just in case.

Each day the dance is the same. A book on the table after breakfast, her review of it at dinner. By the second month, she can see him salivating as he sits, not for the feast but for her opinions of his choice, and despite her resistance at giving him even the slightest compliment, she finds his taste improving. There is the story of a king with four sons who is tricked into putting his favorite one to death by the others. There is the tale of a poor family in a village who comes into great wealth and ends up destroying themselves because of it. There is a book about animals taking back the earth. Most of the stories end unhappily, a warning of why men can't be trusted, and she could read these until the end of her days. But the happier she is with the Beast's choices and the more her eyes shine at the dinner table gazing into his, the lighter his selections start to become—a lost boy finds a family on an island; a town in a drought finds a magic recipe for rain; a queen and lowly cook form an unlikely friendship—until, at last, there is one that offends her, about a book-loving, independent girl at odds with a surly, square-jawed prig of a man before she falls for him and becomes his bride.

You think the ending is a happy one? Mei demands, barely seated at dinner.

They are married in true love, the Beast replies.

True love because he is handsome, Mei insists. She hardly knows him.

What else does a girl need in a man to marry him? he asks. What else does she need to know?

That he is there for her. That he understands her. That when she falls, he will catch her.

I offer you all of those things, the Beast says. Would you marry me?

Mei blinks at him.

It is true love because he is handsome, the Beast growls. That is what all girls want.

The next day there is a book about an ugly girl who trades her voice for beauty so she can marry a gorgeous prince, and Mei can't even finish it. She leaves the book abandoned in the garden, spotlit by the sun, where she knows the Beast will see it.

Have I offended you? he asks at dinner.

You think I do not marry you because of how you look, she says. But you are a Beast who holds me hostage and expects love to blossom in return.

And what if I set you free? the Beast asks. Would you marry me then?

What if I do not want to marry? Mei retorts. What if I don't want to find love at all?

To be alone is no victory, the Beast sighs. I've spent my whole life feeling alone.

Well, I'm not like you, says Mei. I am happier on my own.

You were made by a mother and father. You were made by love, the Beast contends. Love is what gave you the name Beauty. It is the seed of who you are. Even if you shield your heart in the hardness of a beast. Love will find you. Like the light of a thousand fairies found me.

Sparkles flicker in his eyes, like the reflection of tiny wings.

Mei gazes at him, her cheeks blushed.

Then her face turns cold.

You know as much of love as you do beauty, she says, and leaves him there alone.

The next day, he doesn't leave a book in the library.

So she climbs the ladders to the highest shelf,

like a mountaineer to a peak, looking for something to call victory, something she's found for herself—

Mei misses a step.

She falls.

Down, down, down to death—

Soft paws catch her, cradle her, as if he's been there all along. In an instant, love floods her chest, love she's been holding back, love she'd forgotten since her mother died, so filled with light and strength it spears through all the darkness of her heart. He was right. Love found her, just in time. And now she will marry him, her beautiful Beast, because he isn't a beast to her, not in his touch, not in anything that matters.

But Mei is thinking only of herself.

As Mei too often does.

She's fallen from a great height. To catch her, he saves his love instead of himself. His back breaks against marble. She hears it snap, like a heart splintered in two.

When she crawls from the Beast's paws, his eyes are wet, the color fading from his cheeks, life held on to by a last shimmering thread, like the edge of a page.

Please. Don't go, she begs.

She kisses his lips, holds him as he shudders—

Shouts echo outside.

A thunder of horses.

She runs to the front of the castle and throws the doors open.

There is Lieu Wei in full armor, with six handsome men on horses, wielding bows and swords. He's rich again, her father. It was only a matter of time. And now he's come to bring her home.

She slams the doors with vengeance, bolts them, seals herself inside.

To the library she runs—

But the Beast isn't where she left him.

Instead, there's a gorgeous brown prince in a gilded suit, looking like he's come to marry her. One of her father's men!

She doesn't hesitate. She grabs the knife from her leg and stabs the stranger in the chest, a brutal blow, before holding him down, demanding to know what he's done with her Beast.

Tell me! she cries. Tell me!

Only when she sees the sheen on the prince's lips where she kissed them, the familiar fire in his eyes, wild with beastly love, does the breath leave his body and her heart dawn to the depths of her mistake.

To look and not see.

She is as guilty as the rest.

In an empty castle, a girl reads her book.

The fairies bring chocolates and tea.

But all she wants is silence.

A silence only broken when she's finished the last page.

She listens, waiting, waiting, for the shuffle of books from the library, ransacked by an invisible hand, before a new one is left on the table for her to find.

She can hear it now.

Ffft. Ffft. Ffft.

Like ghost steps on marble.

Like the falling petals of a rose.

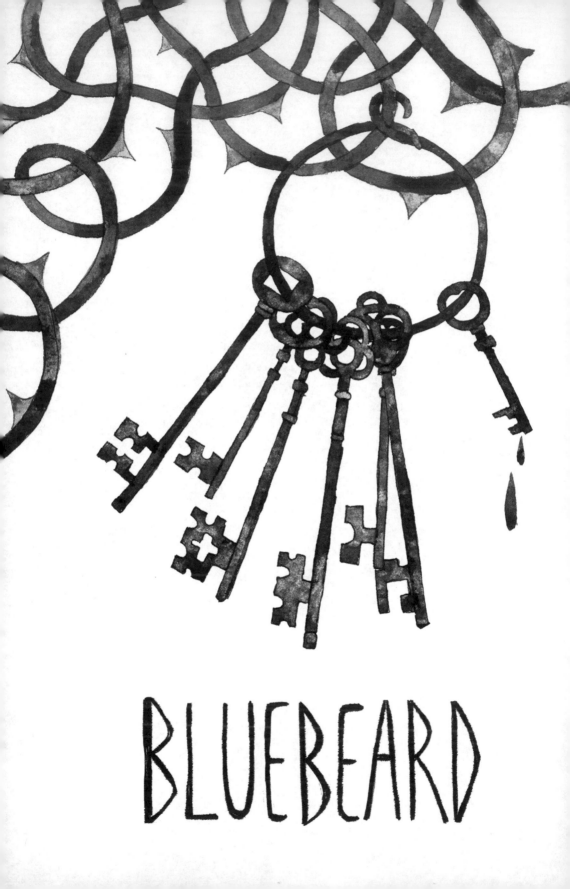

BLUEBEARD

WHEN THE MAN WITH THE BLUE
beard comes, none of the boys want to go with him.

This alarms the master of the orphanage because
every boy craves a home, away from the soggy
beds, pestilent gruel, and ritual beatings that keep
them in line. The misery of the place is designed:
how else to get the boys to scrub their faces and
smile their hardest when the next couple arrives,
a well-meaning man and woman hunting for the
least feral one to call their own?

But the blue-bearded man arrives without
a woman. He strides through the doors alone,
cloaked in a white tiger's skin, his neck and fingers cuffed with rubies, the sharp heel of his black
boots impaling the floor, *clack, clack, clack,* and the
boys have to be threatened with the whip to slink
out of their rooms. They've seen him before. Twice

he's come, lining them up and inspecting each with stone-black eyes and a hollow smile, hunting for something in particular, something he can't quite find, before he leaves empty-handed, the white head of a tiger trailing behind him. He has furry black eyebrows, cropped black hair, and his beard is the color of midnight, so blue and strange that it feels like a warning.

Bluebeard, the boys whisper, conjuring tales as to how this beard came to be: a witch's curse or a dragon's nest or a portal to hell itself. And yet, he does not hide it, instead growing it long and thick, perfectly groomed, like his own private forest. He is as handsome as he is rich. But even so, none of the boys want Bluebeard, even if it means more bondage, more gruel, and for now, Bluebeard doesn't want them.

But then a new boy arrives named Pietro, just turned sixteen, with soft, girlish features and long blond hair and big green eyes that blink like a doll's. It is hard enough to be fresh blood here: the boys have no use for you, not until you've had enough ice-cold baths and worm-infested bowls and giftless Christmases. But Pietro is unholy, with his smooth, pale limbs, tangled eyelashes and wide pink mouth and two small pearls pinned through his ears, as if he isn't much of a boy at all. The others shirk as he passes, especially the older boys, afraid they'll catch whatever it is that makes him less of a man, and yet they can't stop staring, their mouths wet and cheeks blushed. Only young Enzo makes a move and sits next to him at supper, because Enzo notices Pietro isn't eating and thinks if he's nice, he might have his bowl.

Where do you come from? Enzo asks.

Calabria, says Pietro. His voice is airy and sweet, dissipating as it sounds. Boys from the other tables fling spoonsful of gruel at him, catching in his hair. Pietro doesn't mind. They are his brothers, one and all. Made kin by suffering.

Were you in another orphanage? Enzo asks.

No, says Pietro.

Your mother and father died?

When I was nine.

Who did you live with then?

My uncle.

A good man?

For a while.

He gave you up?

Not exactly.

What happened to him?

Pietro turns to Enzo. I killed him.

News like this travels.

Boys stop throwing gruel.

That night, Pietro jolts awake in his bed.

A blue-bearded man reaches out a hand, like an angel in the dark.

None of the other boys are awake, and Pietro thinks he is lost in a dream. But then he sees the orphan master behind the bearded stranger, clutching a sack of gold.

Would you like to come live with me? Bluebeard asks the boy.

Pietro holds his breath.

The same words his uncle spoke when he found him.

Pietro has learned a lot since then.

He knows the dangers of men.

What they keep behind closed doors.

But Pietro is practical.

Every boy here must fend for themselves.

And this is his chance to get out.

Jewels on Bluebeard's fingers glitter in the boy's eyes like wishing stars.

He leans over and kisses them.

Do you have a wife? he asks Bluebeard as they ride in his carriage through the mountains.

The last red ray of sun splits through the window like a saber, leaving the boy drenched in bloody glow and his new master lost in shadow.

I had a wife once, he replies. But wives are curious cats. They nose about and ask too many questions. They are not grateful for what they have. Not like you. You are quiet and obedient. You are grateful to have a man like me protecting you.

There is dominance in his tone, a silencing of Pietro's voice before it can answer. The boy is thankful for the blinding sun, blotting out the face of this man who claims him.

Don't be afraid, says Bluebeard. You may invite anyone you wish to come stay with us. You have family?

No, says Pietro.

Friends?

No.

Ah, then it is just you and I, says Bluebeard.

The light shifts, bringing him out of the dark.
There he is, the portrait of a man, his nose bent
as if it's been broken, a scar on his right cheek not
too old, his skin unnaturally smooth like he's been
embalmed. The smell of him is hard to escape: a
hot, smoky pall, like he's been born out of flames.
Without his fur, the man's meaty arms bulge

through his tunic, the blue of his beard nesting against the dark hair on his chest. He nods at a box of figs, salted almonds, and cheese next to the boy, but Pietro doesn't eat, because to eat is to be owned, like a dog yielding to a collar. Glancing out the window, he watches a forest rush by—kick open the door and he could be gone in seconds—but then he remembers what happens to boys like him who are lost in the woods and always found by men like this. Doesn't matter where he goes. Men like this are everywhere. Vultures pretending to be lions.

The forest passes. In the glass, he sees the man consuming him with a glower. The carriage slows, rolling up the peak toward the castle. Outside, Pietro spots a scrawny old fox, all alone, crouching in the grass. Predators must think he's easy, this fox. Yet he's survived this long, hasn't he? And so has his kind: frail in body but strong of spirit, always up for the chase no matter how many times they're hunted. Because one day they'll be free, free at last to shine their light, free to exist in this world like the wind or the sun or the rain, shaming all weaker hearts who give up too easily. They are brothers, Pietro and this fox, just like Pietro and the boys at the orphanage, every soul that's neglected and underestimated, brothers one and all. Pietro searches deep in the fox's eyes and in his heart, he begins to hear its story, an echo of his own.

The carriage regains its pace. The fox is gone.

What happened to your mother and father? Bluebeard asks.

A flu swept through Calabria, Pietro answers. Only the children were immune. They quarantined the village and didn't let anyone in for months. Most of the children died of starvation. When my uncle came, I was still alive, fed by the slivers of a single stick of butter.

You were lucky, Bluebeard points out.

Pietro looks at him. I was smart.

When Pietro was young, his mother and father used to read him tales of love, about princes with castles who swept girls off their feet, and Pietro used to put himself in the shoes of these girls who started the day ordinary and ended it in a strapping boy's arms. They also read him tales of warning, about handsome men with a past, men who cut their wives' throats, and sometimes Pietro wondered if these tales were one and the same—that the swaggering princes who stole innocent girls to their castles grew into the soulless men that murdered them.

Bluebeard's castle balances on a bluff, three towers of stone with sharp-pointed turrets, like a pitchfork rising out of the sea into the dark night sky. As the carriage curls through the gates and up the mountain drive, Pietro hears the waves smashing against the rocks, like the roars of ghosts battering a door. There are no stablemen, no butlers waiting. The driver rides the carriage away. When Bluebeard leads Pietro into the castle, they are all alone.

The first thing Pietro sees is the curved blade of a sword, suspended in darkness like a gleaming smile. Then light floods his view, a hundred chandeliers, mirrorballs of flame and crystal, illuminating the sword on a wall and long hallways to either side, paved with red velvet, a path to stay on. The house smells of its keeper, that thick, smoky musk, and Pietro surrenders to it, taking full breaths as he moves past the sword and explores the house without asking. It is a wonderland of flowers and candy, blooms of violets, oleanders, bougainvillea in each room, alongside tins of chocolate, marzipan, and frosted crepe cakes. Caskets and chests and closets abound, many of them locked, gleaming with shiny keyholes that Pietro wants to peek through. Dolls keep watch like sentinels, china girls and boys, perched on beds, seated on cushions, packed into glass cases, their stares on the boy wherever he goes. Bluebeard is there too, tracking him like a shadow. Their eyes meet in a mirror.

Which is my room? Pietro asks.

All of them, says Bluebeard. Except one.

Pietro returns a quizzical glance, but his keeper is already down the hall, the thin red carpet carrying him like a stream of blood. Bathe and put fresh clothes on, Bluebeard orders. There are some in every closet for you. Dinner is in twenty minutes.

Pietro finds a bathtub next door already filled with steamy water, pink-coated bubbles, and sprinkles of cherry blossoms. He locks himself in and slips out of the clothes he's been wearing for days, studying his dirty, humbled face in the mirror before he sinks underwater, into roaring silence, wondering if this is the last time he'll be free. Once he and his new master sit at the dinner table, the hunt will begin.

Pietro learned this with his uncle.

Stages of a hunt.

First stage, the deal.

I take care of you and you be a good boy.

Second stage, the threat.

Betray me and you'll be in the streets.

Third stage, punishment.

The deal is broken.

Things can't go back to the way things were.

Death slicks the way in every direction, like oil awaiting a flame.

Pietro opens a closet and finds a silk shirt, pure and princely blue. He pairs it with a pair of white linen pants, and when he looks in the mirror, he's like a crisp summer's sky. There was no mention of where dinner would be served, so he wanders the halls until he smells the bloody fragrance of meat and finds Bluebeard waiting at a long glass table pressed against more glass overlooking the sea, the surface reflecting the alien blue of his beard and his black velvet coat, with two plates of steak, potatoes, and peas and coffers of chocolates laid out on either side of a tall, dripping candle.

Pietro picks around the meat.

Bluebeard watches him and smiles.

Tomorrow I will go to Astapol on business, he says. I'll be gone at least two weeks. But this will give you time to get comfortable in your new home. There is plenty of food in the kitchen, though I can see you won't require very much.

Pietro goes to pick a chocolate out of the coffer—

Bluebeard flicks it shut.

Listen to me, he says starkly.

Pietro lifts his eyes.

The deal.

From his coat, Bluebeard pulls a ring of keys and lays it on the table, a loop of polished steel, the keys splayed out from it like a hundred sharp teeth.

These are the keys to all the rooms in my castle, he says. Rooms that you have full permission to enter and claim. And not just the rooms. The closets and caskets and strongboxes of jewels. All of them are yours. But there is a little one there, small and black. Do you see it now?

Pietro eyes the tiny black key, apart from the others, smooth as obsidian, like it's made of something deeper than metal, from the core of the earth.

That is the only key you're not allowed to use, Bluebeard warns. It opens a chamber in the basement of the north tower. I forbid you to go into that chamber, and if you do, you will be severely punished.

How clear, Pietro thinks, watching the tempestuous sea. Usually the stages of a hunt rise on the tides, but here they come together, like keys on the same ring, deal, threat, punishment, one, two three.

Take the keys, Bluebeard orders. They are yours now.

Pietro has no choice.

The game has already begun.

At dawn, Bluebeard departs for Astapol. He knocks at Pietro's room before he goes, curling his head inside, but Pietro pretends to be asleep. Cocooned in satin sheets, he waits until he hears the doors to the castle shut before he bounds to the window. Alone, he watches the carriage pull up and absorb the bulk of the man with his small suitcase before the horses ride him down the mountain into ink-blue light.

Pietro exhales.

For six days, he is in heaven. He struts about the castle in Bluebeard's furs, in fancy suits and tall-heeled boots, in velvet smoking jackets and cottony robes, eating chocolates and cake and draping himself over the couch like a bored queen, reading the romances that he finds on the shelves. When it is warm, he goes outside and sunbathes on the lawn or dances on the roof to imaginary music or makes himself a picnic of melon and yogurt and cornichons, imagining he is at a country palace all his own. At night, he invents new recipes and takes his time cooking them—spicy mango ginger soup, mushroom risotto with truffle oil, ratatouille with sunchokes, couscous with pomegranate and lentils—before eating them in silence, reveling in the taste even if it is terrible, after which he cleans the kitchen to a spotless shine so that tomorrow he can do it all again. Each night, he sleeps in a different room, and it feels like he will never run out of them.

But then the creeping feeling comes, that tightness in the neck, the reminder that he is still owned, like a lamb left to gorge and play before it learns why it's been bought. That feeling grows and festers until he's at breakfast in a robe, a towel around his head, his skin smelling like white orchids, his belly filled with coconut cream, and yet he can think of nothing but the key in his pocket, *that* key, the one he's supposed to forget about. The deal is simple: do not breach the north tower basement and he will go unpunished. A simple test of curiosity. Most boys would fail such a test, too tempted by transgression, but he is not most boys. To him, it is a trifling rule to obey in exchange for this kind of life, where he can lord about a mountain manor and howl at the moon.

The phantom vise around his neck draws tighter. Except this life *isn't* real, of course. Bluebeard will return, and Pietro won't be master of the castle anymore. He'll be its slave. That is the deal he made when he took Bluebeard's hand. Save himself from the orphanage, even if he couldn't save the others. Freedom at any cost.

But how can you live by a deal if you don't know its price?

Up from the table and down to the chamber he goes in a single breath, still in his robe and turban, acting as if this is a lark, like a trip to the cellar for more olive oil or an extra set of blankets. But inside, his stomach is churning, his muscles hot with adrenaline, like he's a fox about to be chased.

The basement is sparse, nothing lying about except a tall rack of wine and a few locked chests, but for a basement, it is well-kept and clean, and Pietro wonders if he is in the wrong tower, because he doesn't see a door—

Until he does.

Because only one who is looking for it would find it, hidden in shadow at the far end. As Pietro approaches, he can see the floor near the frame is darkly stained and carved with deep footprints, as if the memories of those who stepped here cannot be erased. This is his last chance to turn back, but he won't, for this is the path, the only door to the truth, and pulling the ring from the pocket of his robe, his fingers find the smooth black key and slip it into the lock. He turns it sharply, the door unbolting, and he drags the heavy weight open—

He lets out a shout and topples against the door, the key falling from his hands and clanging onto stone.

Six boys prop against the chamber walls,

different in height, size, shade of skin, but all his age, with the same soft features and ethereal lightness, like they do not answer to the call of boy or girl. Their throats are slashed, their clothes stained with blood, their eyes wide open, as if they each witnessed the horror of this room but could not avoid its fate.

Pietro clutches his neck, his breath sucked away. He needs to get out—now, *now*, now!—before he leaves any sign or trace. Panicked, he snatches the keys from the floor, only to find a splotch of blood marking the one to this room. He scrubs it with his hand, but it does not go. He runs upstairs, drowns the key in water and soap, douses it with bleach and oil, sets fire to it on the stove, but it remains unchanged, the red stain indelible, brighter with each attempt to erase it. What to do? Hide it? Get rid of it? But what if Bluebeard asks for it? Of course he will ask! Then he'll find the bloodspot, the spot that won't come out, because it isn't meant to come out—

It dawns on him.

Just like it must have dawned on six boys before.

Deal, threat, punishment.

Stages of a hunt.

The deal has been broken.

The threat unheeded.

Now he will die.

Unless he slips out now, down the mountain and into the trees, run, run, run—

A roar of sound outside.

Pietro sprints to a window. A carriage swerves up the road from the base of the mountain, a shadow lit by two torch flames like the glare of a demon. Bluebeard is on his way, sensing the boy's crime the same way he sensed his arrival to the orphanage.

There is no escape.

Pietro drops to his knees, sobs strangling him, as he thinks of the monster coming to kill him, of the empty plot of stone on the wall next to the others where he will lie—

Slowly, his cries soften.

His breaths steel.

The story is not over yet.

Even though it's been told before.

Each boy thinking they're different.

Each boy thinking they could break the rules of men.

Each brought to slaughter.

But Pietro *is* different.

Because Pietro doesn't just fight for himself.

He fights for his brothers.

And those who fight for others don't go down so easily.

His uncle learned that lesson well.

He thought he had Pietro beaten, cornered for life.

Three drops of poison, added to Uncle's wine . . .

Foxes find a way.

Now he returns to the bloody chamber.

This time, he stands tall as he opens the door, the key firm between fingers.

Once inside, he takes his time, bending down to the first corpse and gazing into scared eyes, touching his cold, dark skin as if Pietro is there with him at death's stroke, holding him through the fear. Pietro kisses him on the forehead, a kiss to bond them in brotherhood and love, and in return, he hears the boy's story in his heart.

Bluebeard enters his castle, bloodlust and thunder.

He's grinning, the white crescent shining in the

dark like the sword on the wall that greets him. He pulls the blade down into his fists. Then he goes to hunt.

He doesn't need to see the key.

He doesn't need evidence.

He can taste the blood in his mouth.

This is what he lives for.

Catch and kill.

Only there is no sign of him.

The boy.

Bluebeard never thinks of them by their names.

No one in the bedrooms or closets. No one hiding under a bed.

Most hide under the bed.

So where is he?

He remembers one boy who never left the forbidden chamber, too scared to hide, waiting for his punishment with the bodies of the others. That's how soft and gentle he was. This boy reminds him of that one, with his lioness hair and guileless eyes.

The door in the basement is still open.

He can see the boy's footprints, fresh in the floor.

Gently, he pushes into the room—

Bluebeard stiffens.

They're gone.

All gone.

The chamber is empty, nothing left but blood.

Now he's on the move, his boots clattering up the steps, his sword tight in his fist, his breaths caught like he's the one being chased. He sprints to the top of the stairs, into the west wing, following the red path through torchlit halls, until at last he reaches that room made of glass, overlooking the bluffs—

They're here.

Waiting for him.

Six boys, seated for dinner.

Shirts torn open.

Names painted in blood on their chests.

Alistair, who loves cats.

Rowan, who loves chocolate.

Lucas, who loves the ocean.

Stefan, who loves to run.

Pedro, who loves horses.

Sebastian, who loves to sing.

Bluebeard makes a choking sound, like he can't find air, his cheeks turning the color of his beard.

In a storm, he dashes to each one, smearing at the blood, trying to scrub it out, but he only makes it worse, lurching from one boy to the next, the blood staining his face, his arms, his beard, until he gets to Sebastian and claws at him, scours at his chest, trying to purge him and his name, only to feel something else there, something behind him, as if his body is guarding another's. Bluebeard grabs Sebastian, shoving him aside—

A seventh boy waits.

Blood bright on his skin.

Pietro, who loves his brothers.

Bluebeard raises his sword—

Pietro stabs him in the heart with a steak knife and smashes him with a chair, into the window, into the glass, shattering it all, before the master tumbles, eyes wide open, into the great savage sea.

The orphanage master works late into the night, listening for the sound of mischief from the beds, so he can have a boy to whip.

Outside, the wind gathers force, the beginning of a storm.

Then an echo of boots, *clack, clack, clack.*

The door is thrown open.

A man in a white tiger's fur.

The orphanage master stands.

Bluebeard, he thinks.

More gold to be had.

But as the man approaches, the orphanage master sees he has no beard. He is smooth and slim, hair to his shoulders, a hat shadowing his face. He carries a large chest, which he drops at the orphanage master's shoes like a stone and kicks ajar.

The orphanage master's eyes shiver, reflecting a trove of diamonds and jewels.

I am here for a boy, says the stranger.

The orphanage master gapes back, his voice a stutter: Which . . . which boy?

The stranger lifts his face into the light.

Pietro smiles.

All of them.

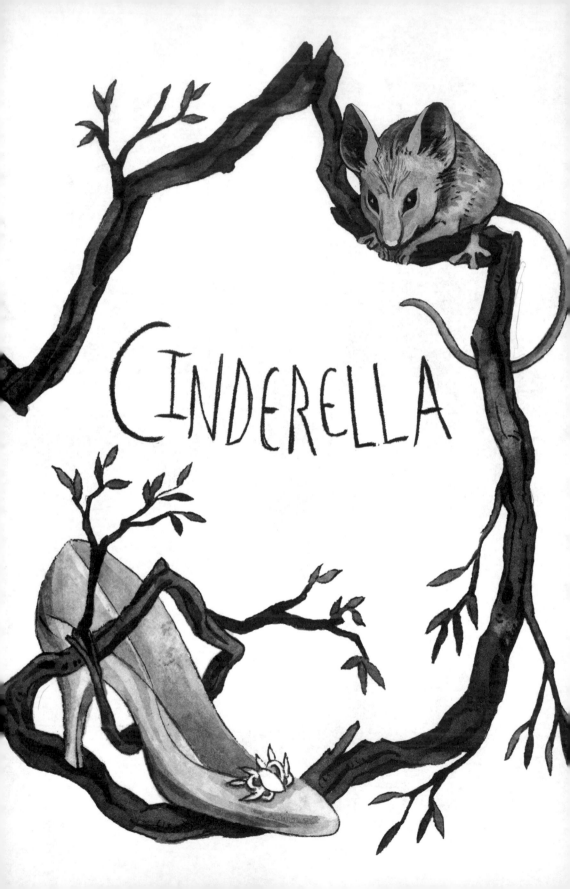

SIX MONTHS AGO, MAGDALENA HAD plans to marry a handsome prince, but then she was turned into a mouse.

These things happen, when you are the most charming girl in Málaga and a gorgeous prince named Dante with bronze skin and windswept hair happens upon you during his tour of the coast while you are selling green cantaloupes at the market. At the time, he'd been engaged to Princess Inez, but that was an arrangement of convenience, and the moment Dante set eyes on Magdalena and her melons, Inez was cast to the wind. Unfortunately for Magdalena, Inez was also a witch and punished Magdalena for stealing her prince by turning her into the white little mouse that she is now.

After the cursing, Magdalena scurried all the

way to Madrid, to Dante's castle, to explain to the prince that she had not died in a fire—which is what Inez told him—and that she could still marry Dante and be his princess if they could just find a magician to fix things. But mice can't talk, and Dante's stewards were fastidious about their exterminations, and Magdalena was lucky to make it out of the castle alive. So she darted from house to house in surrounding villages, hunting for a safe place to hide until she made a better plan, and that's how she found the home of Cinderella, the only girl in Spain who enjoys the company of rodents.

She is as woeful as her name, this Cinderella, too meek to claim her real name, always dirty-faced and sheepish and acting like a martyr, which her stepmother and two stepsisters take advantage of, even though all of them should be slapped in the face. At this very moment, for instance, Cinderella is washing her stepsister's undergarments at the crack of dawn even though she herself hasn't had a chance to eat or bathe.

And for what, says Magdalena, waving her tiny paws. So you can be ridiculed for smelling like wet rags after? So they can call you Cinderella again and again until it's become your name? They are like two poodles, your stepsisters, with bad hair and fat bottoms, and they spray themselves with so much cheap perfume that I can smell them three rooms away.

Oh, Magdalena, Cinderella sighs, for the girl understands the language of mice. This is the only way to keep peace in this house. My stepmother loathes me, and my father loves her more than me. I don't mind it, to be honest. Housework keeps me busy, and the place stays clean. There isn't much else to do.

Not much else to do! the mouse starts. Your father is rich. Steal some of his gold and go cheer the bull runs in Pamplona or shop the Portal de l'Àngel or sunbathe on Ibiza sands—

And besides, Cinderella cuts in sternly, my mother used to say: Be virtuous and kind and good things will come to you.

And what good did it do her? She died young and then her husband married a viper, Magdalena retorts.

This Cinderella has no response to, but the

mouse does notice that she rubs her sister's panties against the washboard with a bit more force.

Magdalena doesn't have much respect for the girl, because she is prettier than Magdalena ever was, with that heart-shaped face and doe-brown eyes, but Magdalena had wiles and wit and a sense of fashion and never would have gotten herself into a situation where she was treated like the maid in her own house, slaving for sisters not related to her by blood. Yet perhaps Magdalena was too smart a fox, because that's how a poor girl from Málaga ended up tempting a prince while all the other poor girls in town married boys with missing teeth or warts on their toes. But poor girls shouldn't tempt princes, because that's the lore of fairy tales, and fairy tales always have a witch. Now Inez is set to wed Prince Dante and Magdalena hasn't told Cinderella that her pet mouse is, in fact, Prince Dante's true love. And she certainly can't tell her now, because all of a sudden, Cinderella is convinced *she* has a chance of marrying Dante instead of Inez.

The problems began when the invitations arrived, smelling of Dante's rugged cologne and requiring the presence of all unmarried women from age sixteen to twenty at his castle two nights before his nuptials, no exceptions allowed.

Clearly he doesn't want to marry Inez, Cinderella pointed out. What kind of prince invites eligible girls to a ball right before his own wedding?

A kind of prince still looking for me, Magdalena thinks to herself, sniffing the invitation, drinking in his scent. He must not believe Inez's story about me dying in a fire. Which means I still have a chance if I get to that ball and show him I'm alive. Then he'll make Inez undo the curse and turn me back into his bride!

Only two problems, of course.

Magdalena is a mouse.

And every eligible girl from here to Galicia has the same thought as Cinderella—that the handsomest prince in all of Spain, who is about to be married, is in fact looking for a different wife.

A ball, Cinderella keeps saying dreamily.

Yes, a ball, Magdalena grumps back.

What to do? It's been three days since the invitations came, with only a week left until Dante's ball, and Magdalena drowns her nerves in a cube of butter. She can hardly think, with those two stepsisters—Bruja and Bruta, she calls them—cackling like hyenas and prattling about the gowns and feathers they will wear and how Prince Dante will fall madly in love with them—which Magdalena can assure them won't happen, even if he was blind and deaf—and her irritation is worsened by the stepmother in her black furs and white hive of hair, like a queen skunk, encouraging her daughters' fantasies even though her disappointment with them is so clearly carved into her face. Perhaps that is why the stepmother is cruel to Cinderella, for Cinderella is the only girl a man could want from this house and she is the daughter of another mother. But these thoughts are distractions from Magdalena's mission. She needs to get to the ball and make her presence known to Dante. Which means she needs an unwitting puppet who will convey her words to her prince . . . someone who can *understand* her, and there is only one person in all of Spain who—

The mouse's eyes flare, her mouth smeared with butter, and she looks straight at the soot-covered girl.

What? Cinderella asks, hunched under the fireplace, sewing sequins on her stepsister's gown. What is it?

Magdalena stands proud on little legs.

We shall go to the ball, she says.

We? Cinderella eyes the mouse. Why would *you* want to go to a ball?

To help you win your prince, of course, Magdalena says, eating her guilt.

With a week to go, there is much to do to prepare Cinderella because she needs to be beautiful enough to get Dante's attention but not so beautiful that he falls in love with her and forgets about Magdalena. This is a delicate balance.

Ow! Ow! says Cinderella, when the mouse plucks more of

her brow. This is ridiculous! A prince won't marry the girl with the nicest eyebrows. He'll marry a girl he can talk to! A girl who is good inside!

You have a fundamental misunderstanding of men, says Magdalena. Now we wax the mustache.

How a lovely girl has let herself languish in disarray this long is a tragedy, but the mouse cleans her up with a good clay mask, a thorough trimming of flyaway hairs, and five days of nothing but watermelon and sweet potatoes to make her glow like an evening star, until at last, she is something to behold, and they can finally think about what she's going to wear.

How about a kimono of gold lamé or a dress with live butterflies hidden in the bosom? Magdalena mulls, sketching outfits in ash with her paw. The ball is tomorrow night. We need something exotic or something extravagant or—

Something like this?

Cinderella's voice floats from the corner.

She holds a silver gown like the sheath of an angel, shimmering silk satin with a bow at the back. It is so simple and beautiful that Magdalena can't breathe.

Definitely *not* that, says the mouse.

And why not? Cinderella asks, surprised.

Because the moment Dante sees you in it, I will join that witch Inez in the trash heap, Magdalena thinks.

Because silver is the color of vulgar women, she says out loud, suddenly feeling like a witch herself. Where did you even get it?

It was my mother's, Cinderella says.

Oh, the mouse peeps.

Cinderella will wear the dress.

But while Magdalena worries about how bright Cinderella should shine, she's forgotten about those who keep her in the dark. The day of the ball, Cinderella's stepmother takes one look at the girl, with her rosy complexion and hopeful smile and magnificent gown freshly steamed, and puts her to work cleaning horse dung in the barn and only once she finishes will she get time to bathe and dress and join their carriage.

Don't do it, Magdalena warns. It's a trap.

Silly mouse, Cinderella sighs.

She works quickly, her clothes and face soiled in manure, and by the time she's done, it is nearly dark, so she runs from the barn to go and get dressed, only to find her sisters and stepmother already in the carriage, the footman about to lock them in. Sister Bruja wears a sequined horror. Sister Bruta wears Cinderella's silver gown.

Cinderella gasps.

Looks better on her anyway, says Stepmother.

Cinderella tears up. But . . . but . . .

The carriage speeds off, leaving a trail of dust.

When it clears, a little white mouse waits for her on the big, empty road, quietly shaking its head.

The girl needs a miracle, but Magdalena is only a mouse.

Ohhh, Santa Theresa, the mouse says, praying into its paws. Please get me and Cinderella to the ball.

Saints don't listen to sinners, says Cinderella.

Since when am I a sinner? the mouse asks.

Since you steal food from the kitchen, drink wine out of my father's best bottles, pepper our conversations with appalling language, and purposely use my stepmother's boudoir as your toilet each morning, Cinderella replies.

The bigger sin is your stepmother using a boudoir each morning and coming out looking like *that*, says Magdalena.

I'm not meant to go to the ball, Cinderella despairs. My place is in the home. And besides, Stepmother's right. The dress looks better on my sister.

You'll be happy when they all drink arsenic and you know it, Magdalena snaps. Enough with the pious phoniness and suffering for no cause. Face it. You *want* to go to the ball. You *want* to marry a prince and stuff it in your sisters' faces and at the very, very least, get out of this house where you are treated more like an orphan than its natural-born heir. As for that dress looking better on your sister, I've seen eggs wrapped in bacon that had more grace. So please stop acting the victim, and tell the truth about how you're feeling for once in your life!

Cinderella's face darkens, and she screws her eyes upon the mouse. Well it is too late to go to the ball anyway—

It's not too late! the mouse decries. We need to get to that ball! *I* need to get to that ball. And you might say: Why would a *mouse* need to get to a ball? Well, I have my reasons, just like you have yours. What are you doing?

Wishing upon a star, says Cinderella, gazing out the window. Mother always said if you are kind and loving, a fairy godmother will arrive when you need her most.

Mouse and girl wait.

No help arrives.

Then a rush of wheels on stone, a carriage bounding past—

Fairy godmother! Cinderella cries, chasing for it.

For a moment, even Magdalena is a believer and scrambles after her. The mouse leaps onto a wheel, then the chassis, vaulting onto the driver's face, making him swerve to a stop, giving Cinderella enough time to throw open the carriage door and jam inside, at which point the mouse abandons the driver and drops through the hole behind him into the passenger car, straight onto Cinderella's lap.

An old squat woman with a babushka around

her head and a black mole that takes up half her
face squints hard at the girl.

Please, Fairy Godmother, can you take me to
Prince Dante's castle? Cinderella begs. There's a
ball, and I simply must go—

I am not your fairy godmother, says the woman,

in a severe accent that is more Moscow than Madrid. I am Svetlana from Varenikovskaya, come to attend Prince Dante's ball myself. But you may ride with me to his castle, since you already have invaded my transportation with that dirty mouse on your lap and your smell of manure. What is your name?

They call her Cinderella, Magdalena blurts, forgetting she's a mouse.

I see. In my country, we call such girls Zolushka, says Svetlana. Girls made of ashes.

Wait . . . you *understand* me? the mouse asks.

Naturally. I am a witch, Svetlana answers. I come to Prince Dante's ball because he is marrying my granddaughter Inez. She is worried he wants another girl and is using this ball as an excuse to find her and call off the wedding. Inez begged me to attend tonight and keep an eye on any maiden who strays too close to her prince. And believe me, if there is a girl he is after, the moment I set eyes on her, she will be turned into a cockroach or a prune. I will do anything for my granddaughter.

The witch's face gnarls with resolve, and the

mouse emits a nervous fart. The last time Magdalena crossed paths with a witch, she ended up like this, and now she's trapped in a carriage with that witch's family! But Svetlana doesn't sense the mouse is in fact Dante's true love. Instead, the witch studies Cinderella as the threat, a good long while, before she leans back in her seat.

I don't worry about you, Zolushka. As beautiful as you are, you have an air of persecution and spinelessness. It is nothing a prince will like.

The mouse peers up at Cinderella, all of its advice to her now confirmed by a second opinion. Cinderella ignores them both, her focus out the window.

Meanwhile, Magdalena mulls the plan. Get Prince Dante to notice Cinderella . . . then use Cinderella to make him realize his cherished melon girl from Málaga is still alive . . .

Part of Magdalena wishes she could just *tell* Cinderella the truth: that she is Dante's true love in a mouse's body; that she is using Cinderella to win him back; that for a girl insistent on doing good deeds, this will be Cinderella's best deed of all. But never once has Cinderella wanted something for herself until the day she saw that ball invitation, and Magdalena feels sorry dashing the poor girl's dreams just when she's finally given herself permission to have them. And yet, she has no choice. Magdalena is in the terrible position of being the one to help Cinderella's dreams of a prince come true—well, *almost* true—before she takes that prince for herself.

The palace approaches, a moonlit alcazar with luminous white and green tile, cascading creepers hung between split-level mezzanines, and long reflecting pools flanked by bitter orange trees. A mob of girls in dazzling gowns exit their carriages, flapping fans in the heat as they wait their turn to be announced inside, while greeting each other with once-over looks and befriending those least likely to be competition. From the carriage window, Cinderella watches them, entranced, while Magdalena shudders, realizing that she's pinned her hopes of winning back her prince to a poo-smelling girl in a ragged house frock without a stitch of lipstick.

She can't go looking like this, can she? the mouse frets, glancing at the witch and gesturing toward

Cinderella. You're a witch, aren't you? Can't you at least give her a proper dress?

Asking a witch to do a good deed, eh? Svetlana chuckles. I'll make you and your Zolushka a deal. You two keep an eye out for any girls poaching my granddaughter's prince and in return, I'll make Zolushka so beautiful no one will hold a candle to her.

Cinderella and the mouse exchange glances.

Deal, they say.

She waves her hands around Cinderella's head, chanting *vaha prada, vaha prada,* then—poof!—a cloud of gold smoke erupts and Cinderella is shiny and new in a frost-blue gown with a crystal-sewn bodice, a lace-embroidered waist, and a cascade of tulle. Glass slippers fit delicately on her feet. She looks like a snow queen, her hair tied in a luscious French twist, her face painted to gilded glow, her skin smelling of peaches and milk.

The spell will only last until midnight, says the witch. That way, if you think about stealing my granddaughter's prince, you'll be back to your *old* self before you ever get the chance.

It is nearly ten already, the mouse thinks. Once

inside, they'll have to move quickly. . . .

And don't you want to look nice for the ball too, little mouse? the witch coos.

A wave of her hands and—poof!—Magdalena is in a tiny white cap and white tuxedo, with bronze buttons and a red bow tie.

Midnight goes for you too, so stay on task, she warns the rodent. Now come, it's time we met my granddaughter.

"Presenting Countess Svetlana and Lady Zolushka of Varenikovskaya!" The monocled footman waves them in, and the witch and Cinderella parade down the staircase and into the candlelit ballroom, a thousand beautiful girls in bold colors, lioness yellow, serpent green, flamenco red, waiting for their turn to dance with Dante, the only man in the room. Magdalena pokes her tiny head from Cinderella's bun of hair; she can't see her prince yet, his waltzing figure obscured by the mob of girls trying to catch his attention, but she spots Inez as the witch leads them toward her, the girl as malnourished and sourpussed as Magdalena remembers, with a bony frame, thin lips, and overplucked eyebrows.

I see what you mean about brows, Cinderella whispers to the mouse.

Inez greets her grandmother with a wail and a hug, ignoring Svetlana's guest.

He hasn't paid attention to me all evening, Granmama! she mewls. He just dances from girl to girl, like he's looking for someone! Someone he wants to marry instead of me!

Well then, we need to find the tramp first and make sure she leaves here stuck to the bottom of your shoe! Svetlana huffs. We are a family of witches. Nothing stops us. The stakes are too high to waste time whining and flapping around like a goose, so use your eyes to find the one he's looking for!

Right then, Inez zeroes in on Cinderella.

And who is *this?* Inez prompts.

Zolushka, says Svetlana. She rode in my carriage. She'll help us find whoever dares claim your prince.

Inez shoots Cinderella a suspicious look. Magdalena tenses so hard a button pops off her tux, spits out of Cinderella's hair, and smacks Inez in the nose.

Let's split up, Cinderella says quickly. We'll search the other side of the ballroom and tell you if we see anything.

She sifts into the crowd of girls.

Good work, Magdalena whispers, peeking out. Think we lost them.

And found something worse, says Cinderella.

Because right in front of them are Bruta, Bruja, and dreaded Stepmother, pushing their way through the pack. It is the first time Magdalena has heard Cinderella speak poorly of them, but Bruta hijacking her mother's dress seems to have stripped the veneer off the girl's good graces. The sisters toss Cinderella a frowning glance, then go back to clamoring for Prince Dante's attention.

They don't even recognize me, Cinderella marvels.

Magdalena's tangled in nerves. Two witches behind them. Three more witches here. They're surrounded by bad women.

Madame?

It is the monocled footman, leaning in.

Prince Dante would like to dance with you.

Me? Cinderella and the mouse say at once.

You, speaks a voice behind the footman.

Prince Dante grins, and a thousand girls freeze around him, like statues in a garden, their eyes on Cinderella. Magdalena wants to leap out of Cinderella's hair, right onto Dante's golden face, with his thick brows and dimpled chin and sparkling white teeth, and smother all of it with kisses, the way she used to, but instead, he's clasping Cinderella's hand, like he's forgotten Magdalena ever existed, and he sweeps the girl and her glass slippers into a waltz.

Your name is Zolushka, Prince Dante says. Where do you come from?

Cinderella is too hypnotized to speak. Magdalena wants to punch her prince in the nose. But then the mouse feels the sweat off Cinderella's scalp, hears the stuttered clink of her shoes, unable to flow with the dance. She is no match for Dante, who can make even the most self-assured girl wobbly. Magdalena takes her chance.

The melon stand in Málaga, the mouse whispers. Tell him you come from the melon stand in Málaga.

What? Cinderella whispers.

Say it! the mouse orders Cinderella.

The girl's too addled by Prince Dante's beauty to come up with anything else—

The melon stand in Málaga, Cinderella croaks.

Eh? Prince Dante says.

Tell him you like your oysters in chorizo butter, Magdalena presses.

Cinderella resists, and the mouse tugs her hair—

I like my oysters in chorizo butter! Cinderella yelps.

Prince Dante's waltz slows, his eyes narrowing.

Mmm ... do I know you? he breathes.

Tell him you like to kiss under the Caminito del Rey, Magdalena whispers.

Cinderella drowns in Prince Dante's eyes.

I like to kiss under the Caminito del Rey.

Dante stops the dance. The ballroom loses all sound, like the silence between tides.

Magdalena? Is it you?

Cinderella stiffens with a shocked whisper: Magdalena ...

It *is* you, then, Dante rasps. There were rumors Inez is a witch ... and I knew ... I knew she'd done something. ...

His hands are around Cinderella's waist. He smiles blindingly, like he's come alive, searching her, searching for the Magdalena inside, and as he wets his lips and bends down, he closes his eyes to kiss his true love, two girls in one, softly, tenderly, until he tastes a mouthful of fur and jolts back, seeing it's not the girl he's kissed, but a mouse straddling her nose. The mouse vaults onto Dante's face, slathering him with more kisses. The prince flails at it, shouting bad words in Spanish—

A slash of red light rips past them.

MOUSE! a voice screams.

Inez, eyes wild, face flushed, points her bony finger at Dante's face.

MOUSE! she screams again, raging for prince and rodent, shooting flaming spells at them both, while grandmother Svetlana chants curses that magically punch holes in the tiles around Prince Dante, aiming to plunge him into oblivion.

All around, girls echo MOUSE! MOUSE! MOUSE!, the worst word to scream at a ball, and they stampede for the exits like mice themselves, debutantes gone rogue, bashing into Prince Dante without care, knocking him and the vermin from his nose onto the imploding floor. Magdalena dances around craters, dodging red spells fired at her tiny head, until soft hands scoop her up and drop her in a pocket, her body tumbling in the dark before she feels a cool gust of wind and thrusts her head out to see Cinderella ushering her through royal gardens toward roads beyond the palace.

Magdalena starts: Cinderella—

Cinderella shoves her into the pocket. Stay down.

Her tone is cold, angry.

I'm sorry— Magdalena says.

You've been Prince Dante's true princess all this time? Hexed in a mouse's body? Cinderella seethes. How could you not tell me!

I never thought you'd believe it! Magdalena admits. And you looked so happy to go to the ball. . . .

I would have been happier knowing I could help you, says Cinderella. If he's your prince, then you belong with him. I'd never stand in the way of love. I'd have helped you instead of being played for a fool.

Magdalena blushes. Must you always be so good?

Cinderella glowers down at the mouse. You were my only friend, Magdalena. And you lied to me. Right now, I don't feel good about you at all.

For once, Magdalena has nothing to say in return.

Cinderella spots her father's carriage atop a steep road and hustles toward it. The driver is gone, the horses idling. Quickly, Cinderella jumps onto a horse—

Well if it isn't Prince Dante's pet, a voice drawls.

She turns to see Bruta and Bruja approaching,

with Stepmother between them.

And now she's trying to steal our carriage, says Bruta.

Does Prince Dante know you're a thief? says Bruja.

Probably in borrowed clothing too, says Bruta.

Now, now, don't be too hard on a stranger, says Stepmother. She can't help pretending to be what she's not. I see it in her eyes. Thinks she deserves a prince. An impostor playing princess. And yet, the more I look at her, the more she reminds me of someone. . . . Yes, our housemaid, Cinderella, who thought she could win a prince's heart too . . . Wouldn't that be something. If Cinderella turned up *here*, playing dirty little tricks. But that would be impossible, wouldn't it? Because we put Cinderella in her place.

She pins her eyes on the girl in front of her.

Just like we will you.

Behind Stepmother, the carriage driver marches toward Cinderella with three sword-armed guards itching to punish the thief.

Cinderella peeks at Magdalena in her pocket. With a single glance, a plan is exchanged. The mouse slides out of its hiding place, under the girl's armpit, onto the landing between horse and carriage . . .

Nothing to say for yourself? the stepmother taunts.

Slowly the girl raises her eyes. Looks right at the woman.

My name isn't Cinderella, she says. It's *Lourdes*.

Behind her, a mouse pulls a bolt, detaching carriage from horse, and the chassis runs backward, smashing Bruja, Bruta, and the mother who made them, rolling all three down the hill.

The mouse ejects just in time, hopping into Lourdes's hands before the girl sprints up the slope, driver and guards chasing. Lourdes grips Magdalena, stumbling over cobblestones in glass slippers, losing both shoes as she crests the hill—

She stops cold.

Inez and Svetlana wait for her.

Grim reapers, young and old.

One girl, two witches.

This is her lot in life.

Outnumbered by the wicked.

Good, without reward.

For the first time, she loses faith . . .

. . . just as death flies at her heart.

Red spells sizzle like devil horns.

A white ball of fur leaps from Lourdes's hand—

Curses impale the mouse instead of the girl.

Somewhere a clock strikes midnight.

Magic ended.

Old selves returned, like a witch promised.

Magdalena falls, a mouse no longer.

Beast turned to beauty, caught in a cinder girl's arms.

Magdalena? Lourdes whispers.

Lourdes . . . , Magdalena breathes.

Lourdes holds her, comforts her, tends to the last spark of life inside her, stoking it brighter, stronger than any prince's kiss.

But the witches aren't done. They raise their hands to cast a fatal blow at the soot-faced girl and the friend she protects—

The blow never comes, their hands caught by guards, back under a prince's command.

Slowly, Lourdes looks up at Dante on his white horse, heroic and imposing, and she holds Magdalena tight as if she's not ready to give her up.

The prince smiles and lifts two glass slippers in his palms, like two wedding rings, as if he has enough love for them both.

⚜

Dante brings two girls to his castle.

It is every prince's dream.

Two to choose from.

Twice the Ever After.

But instead, each morning, it is Magdalena who Lourdes looks for and Magdalena who looks for Lourdes.

In time, Dante grows bored and woos a third, but by then his birds have flown the coop.

They are on their own now, Magdalena and Lourdes, unbound from the rules of happy endings. Like rebels on the run, they search for adventure, for a new place to call home. But youth keeps them moving, to new cities, to new shores, drinking up experience, like they're trying to swallow the sea. Years pass and the wanderings slow; roots take hold. Magdalena gets married and divorced. Lourdes doesn't marry but finds a nice enough man and bears three sons. Their lives change. They grow old. But through it all, nothing stops their friendship, not sickness or heartbreak, not distance or years, not even the specter of death, and in their last days, when they sit together by the fire, hunched and pale, like two frail mice, there is only love between them, as if there is nothing else in this world, as if this is not an ending, but how it was always meant to be.

THE
LITTLE
MERMAID

DO YOU KNOW HIS NAME? THE SEA
witch asks.

No, says the young mermaid.

Does he know yours?

No.

Did you exchange any words whatsoever?

No.

And yet, you want to trade your fins for legs,
disavow your friends and family, pay any price, all
so you can ascend to the upper world and stalk this
prince you do not know and try to get him to love
you, even though he could be a psychopath or a
philanderer or a prince who prefers the company
of men.

The first time I saw him, I knew he was the one
I'm supposed to marry, the girl insists.

That blush in your cheeks, that quiver in your

voice . . . You are confusing passion for love. At your age, I used to get stirred up too. Your father, Drogon, used to kiss me in the kelp forests when we were young, and now he sends his guards to try to kill me twice a month. What seems like love is often desire in disguise. And desire passes. Ask Daddy. Once upon a time, Drogon vowed his love to me, promising I would be his queen. And now I'm banished from his court.

My love for this prince will never pass! the mermaid says. I would die for him.

Don't be tragic. You are a beautiful girl, and the point of beauty is to make people die for *you*. At the very least, tell me what qualities he has that make him husband material.

He is as handsome as the most perfect statue—

Which will fade with time and soon he will be bald, grumpy, and fatter than me. Handsome is not enough. What else.

He is valiant and strong. He could have died during the storm. But he stayed alive as I swam him to shore.

And I'm sure he'll take all the credit for it. Did he even thank you for your help?

old dragon that could use your magical powers for good, but you use them for evil against him and his people, all because he wouldn't marry you. And he says you've made yourself repulsive and a witch just to spite him because everyone knows he used to be with you before my mother.

Drogon . . . said all that?

It's why I could come here without being seen. He doesn't even have guards watching this part of the reef. He assumes none of us would dare consort with the sea witch.

Good to know. And what if I think *you're* the witch?

Me?

Yes.

Do I look like a witch to you?

Imagine this. An old, spinster mermaid, about your mother's age, likes to keep to herself inside her house outside the borders of the kingdom. She doesn't hurt a soul—unless someone comes tres-passing on her property, because the sea king is trying to kill her and she can no longer tell friend from foe. This makes the old mermaid fortress inside her home even more, gorging on whatever scraps and bottom-feeders wash into her polyps while keeping company with eels and snakes and other slithering creatures that relish her decrepit appearance. The old mermaid doesn't mean to look the way she does, but she no longer gets exercise, not with the king's bounty hunters after her, and besides she's grown lonely, and loneliness means she no longer thinks about the possibility of having to vie for self-respect in a room full of others. (Pass the crab claws and scallop soufflé.) Then one murky afternoon, the daughter of the king comes to see the old merwoman. She does not ask for an appointment. She does not knock on any doors. She just barges into the spinster's house, demanding help even though the old spinster is her father's worst enemy. It is clear this girl is a traitor to her family, selfishly seeking out the same person her father aims to kill, but it turns out there are more sins to her name. For one thing, she's been roaming about in the upper world—forbidden by her father's decree—and not only is she disobedient, but she's also reckless, rescuing a prince who sank with his poorly made ship and deserved to die. But it gets worse: she isn't just trespasser and traitor, but now we find out she's fallen in love with this prince based on his looks, since they exchanged no words or thoughts or opinions that might give her credence as to his values, other than a handsome face. So add shallowness to her list of sins. And now, she demands the old spinster grant her wish of marrying this prince, all the while occupying the spinster's home like a thief holding a prisoner hostage without the slightest indication of what she's going to do for the old merwoman in return: no price or gift or even hint of gratitude. Is it any wonder that the spinster backs deeper into her cave, keeping narrowed eyes upon this intruder, this turncoat, this predator, and is tempted to kill her on the spot? For who could hear this story and think the witch could be anything other than the little mermaid herself?

I've blown air bubbles with more truth, the young mermaid retorts. No one would believe that version of the story.

No? Where's the lie? Tell me where I've faltered.

In every good story I've heard, love is the answer, says the mermaid. If you find your one true love, you fight for them. No matter what it costs. That's how you win a happy ending. By being bold and courageous. And by coming to you, I've been both those things, where others might give up and settle for less. Where you see sins, I see goodness.

And what makes me the evil one? her opponent asks. What makes me the witch?

Because you are in my way, says the little mermaid. You are the obstacle to love. Whether you turn out to be fairy godmother or wicked witch . . . I suppose that's up to you.

And yet, if I make it too easy, then you're not *fighting* for love, are you? says the witch.

A girl trying to win her prince . . . It's the greatest fairy tale of all, the mermaid points out. And there's no such thing as a fairy tale that comes easy.

Perhaps we have that in common, then, says the witch. I fought for a prince too. But it didn't earn me a happy ending.

Maybe you didn't fight hard enough, says the mermaid. Or maybe your heart really is evil where mine is good.

Or maybe I saw love where I wished it would be, says the witch. Projecting onto a man what I wished I could give to myself. Making him the answer to everything. Now that is *real* evil.

I think you're projecting onto *me*, the mermaid says.

And yet you stand here, ready to pay a price your man won't pay for you. I would have given up everything for your father, but Drogon wouldn't sacrifice anything for me, not even the slightest chink in his reputation. And why should he? There is nothing more attractive to a man than a girl who silently surrenders her power to him. It is what fairy tales are built upon. Girls who have to pass a test to win a man, tests of pain and suffering, trials of fire, while a man waits on the other side of the flames, yawning and scratching his belly, waiting for one to come through. That is why you're so seduced by this prince, who doesn't know you exist. Because it *feels* like every fairy tale we've ever known. Giving up your self, your soul, your *world* to have him, while he looks handsome and takes credit for your travails. It seems like the path to Ever After, doesn't it? The myth that's been told to girls so many times before. I followed that well-heeled path and here I am, alone in the dark at the end of it. But maybe your story is different than mine. Maybe your father was just the wrong man. As you said, Drogon likes his girls quiet and obedient. That isn't me, and it isn't you. We're two rebels, you and I. Two witches of your father's court. If only I knew the truth before I gave a man so much power. If only I knew my man as well as you think you know *yours.*

I do know my prince, the mermaid rejects. I know he's a good man—

You only know what you see, and you can't see that. To know a man, you must use your voice and ask him the questions I should have asked mine. Will you be faithful? Will you love me for who I am? Will you see me as equal? You don't know those answers. Perhaps you don't care.

Love is felt in the heart, the mermaid claims.

And that means you can't question it? the witch asks.

The mermaid insists: Ask too many questions and . . . and . . .

What? We'll see who they are? A pig instead of a prince? A devil instead of a sea king? How inconvenient.

I-I-I'm not like you, she stutters. You and Daddy . . . My prince is different—

Oh yes, there is definitely a difference between

my Drogon and your prince, says the witch. With all that you're about to give up for him, this true love, this one-and-only, this eternal soul for which you'll mutilate your body and cut short your life . . . you don't even know his *name*.

Silence dawns. Deep as the great, blue sea.

Your new legs. Shall we discuss the price? the witch asks.

The little mermaid holds her voice.

Instead, she looks back toward the mouth of the cave.

THE DEVIL DOESN'T WANT YOU TO know his name.

That is his power, for as long as you don't know his name, he is a fog, a concept, a raging infinite sea that can swallow you up at every corner of the earth. But know his name and that means someone *gave* him that name and suddenly the Devil isn't the Devil but a soul beholden to the one who named him, and isn't that who we should be afraid of? No, no, we can't know his name, otherwise the Devil will have a story, a beginning and an end just like you or me, and Hell has no threat when it is staffed by commoners.

But the Devil also likes to flirt with his own destruction—just like those he recruits to his cause—so he makes it a point to torment the weakest and greediest and guiltiest of the lot in their worst moments of need and make them guess his name. Guess right and live. Fail and burn forever. All of them fail, of course. But it's in good fun! Give the damned a chance. Wink, wink.

There are a lot of sinning fools to choose from, and today, as he hunches over his river Styx, a churning, bubbling bath, each of the bubbles shows him a soul ready to be plucked from their time on earth and whisked down to eternal suffering. He can hear the screams of his choir now, millions strong, broiling in the dungeons beneath his river. Who will join his little chickies? He sings a song, because the Devil is an artist:

Fiddle dee dum, Fiddle dee dee,
Look at my bubbles, one two three.
Who will play my game?
Who will guess my name?
Who will be the next to burn in flames?
A frigid, spoiled girl
Or a boastful father
Or a king with a rapacious eye—

Then he realizes all three are part of the same scene, each as wicked as the other, and now he's curious, so he picks up the bubble into long, crooked claws and slides it to his ear like a seashell to listen in.

I hear you've been telling everyone your daughter is the most beautiful girl in all the land, so I wanted to see her for myself, the king addresses the father.

Isn't she? The father grins, holding the girl close. My fair Mathilde.

Indeed, says the king, wrapped in gold silk robes on a golden throne. I would take her as my wife, except she is but a miller's daughter and unbecoming of a king. Any wife I take must be worth her weight in gold, like the Princess of Habsburg-Lorraine or the Widow Von Du. They are not as lovely as your daughter, of course, but gold lasts longer than good looks. It might be nice having your girl around my castle though. Perhaps she could make a good wife for my nephew Gottesfried.

Consider it done, Your Highness, the father replies. To marry into your court would be the highest honor—

May I see this Gottesfried first? Mathilde cuts in.

The king takes in the gold-tressed girl and her sharp green eyes and upturned nose. You think a nephew of the king is not good enough for you?

If I'm the most beautiful girl in the land, don't you think I deserve a choice? Mathilde responds.

The king frowns and bangs the end of his staff on marble. Bring me Gottesfried!

The doors to court open and the guards escort a smiley boy with small shoulders and a birdlike chest. He's distracted by a butterfly flitting about the gilded ceiling.

Mathilde turns to the king. No, not for me, thanks.

King and father stare at her.

I'll wait for you in our carriage, Father, says Mathilde.

My carriage that *I* sent to receive you— the king starts.

But Mathilde is already gone.

The king turns his glare upon the miller. . . .

Meanwhile, the Devil smiles to himself. Usually there's one noble soul to spoil a story. But not here. With these three, no one can bring it back to God. Haughty girl, spurned king, selfish father . . . A feast of bad behavior. Even the Devil himself doesn't know what will happen next. Though if he had to guess, the miller's about to lose his head—

She can spin straw into gold you know, the miller insists to the king. My daughter. That's why she's so proud. She even spun her own *hair* into gold. Did you notice its sparkle and sheen?

The Devil cackles. Oh, that's good. That's very good.

The king's eyes turn flinty and wide. Ah, I see. I see! Yes, that explains everything. She must be fetched back and stay here overnight. I shall put her to the test . . .

The miller can only smile and nod.

It's Mathilde's problem now.

Let her learn her lesson.

Let them all learn their lesson.

The Devil hops from foot to foot.

The time is coming.

Who will play my game?

Who will guess my name?

Who will be the next to burn in flames?

Mathilde is whisked into a room filled with straw.

A spinning wheel waits in the corner.

Your father told me of your talents, the king
says. It appears you have some value beyond good
looks. So get to work now. Spin all night, and if by
morning you have not spun all this straw into gold,
then you are useless to me and will die.

The king locks the door and leaves her there
alone.

Mathilde sits upon a bale of straw, gazing at the
spinning wheel and a basket of empty spools. For
a while, she thinks this is a cruel joke, a punishment for not marrying that wispy boy, but then she
remembers who her father is and how naturally he
lies. It is why she is so cold inside. When your father
is a thief and a crook and a liar, you must learn to
live without your heart. Instead, she puts her faith
in beauty, spending the days improving her hair, her
skin, her figure, hoping a prince will take notice and
rescue her from her father's grasp. Yet it's her father
who takes the most notice, and he brags all over town
about her looks to any man seeking a wife, hoping
to earn himself a fortune in exchange for selling her,
like she's a milk cow or a precious stone. For a while,
she warded him off, dismissing his lot of hoggish
suitors as unworthy and her father couldn't argue

because it was true. But then he came to her with the king's invitation and she thought maybe he was good for something after all. . . .

Now he has left her in a dire situation. She must spin this straw into gold or die. That she doesn't know how to spin anything is a deeper twist of the knife. Her father always told her she should learn to spin, sew, cook to secure her future, while she bet on beauty as the path out of his clutches. But now he's bartered her to a king who doesn't want her for her beauty at all. Fear fills her up, heating all the parts that are usually cold, and before she knows it, she's crying, which she hardly remembers how to do, and that scares her even more. She should have married Gunther or Goatherd or whatever his name was. But the boy looked like a feckless git who she'd spend her life ignoring, and who wants that for a husband when her beauty deserves the kind of man who captains ships or wrangles lions? No to Geberhardt. Definitely no. But saying no is how she ended up here. Why must everything in life be a bargain!

Then the door opens and a strange little man steps inside.

He has a red glow to his skin, a black mustache, and a black hat. He walks all hunched up, with skinny legs and a lumpy bottom, as if he is hiding a tail inside his breeches. He sets dark eyes upon the girl and says: Hello, Mathilde. Quite a trap you're in. Lucky for you, I can spin straw into gold. So let's play a game.

He smiles jagged little teeth that shine like pearls.

W-w-who are you? Mathilde asks.

But she already knows the answer.

He grabs his hat with long red claws and pops it off, revealing two pointy horns.

The Devil, of course, he says.

Mathilde shudders. What game do you want to play?

I want you to guess my name, says the Devil. And if it's a good guess, then I'll help you.

Mathilde backs away. Playing games with the Devil doesn't seem like a wise thing to do, she says.

What choice do you have? the Devil asks.

To pray to my angels instead, says the girl.

Angels only reward a good girl. Are you good?

Yes.

Then why am I here instead of your angels?

To this, the girl has no answer.

You are not meant for heaven, says the Devil. Maybe it's because you love no one but yourself. Or maybe it's because you cultivate beauty instead of goodness. And don't use your father as an excuse. Plenty of people have worse fathers and have made something of their lives instead of acting hoity-toity and waiting for some prince to rescue them. Then again, your father is so noxious that I'm not surprised you wear the stench of his sins, like your mother did. Good woman on the surface, but to marry a man like your father ... Well, that requires the kind of soul that ends in my clutches. I checked on her before I came. Somewhere in the fifth circle and on her way down. Still thinks she belongs in heaven, poor lass. Those kinds never fare well. The pain is twice as bad when you resist it. What I'm saying is that your soul is going to come to me one way or another like Mummy's did and like Daddy's will, so might as well play my game and try to snatch more time up here where you can keep pretending you're better than everyone else and your angels are guarding you. Do we have a deal? Lovely. Now tell me. What is my name?

Mathilde reddens, about to argue—

The next word out of your mouth I'll take as your answer, says the Devil.

Mathilde swallows whatever she's about to say. She doesn't want to make a deal with the Devil. She doesn't want to admit any of what he's said is true. But she also knows her angels aren't coming. Not if they've let things get this far.

Lucifer? she guesses.

Oh, that is a pitiful guess, the Devil moans. Lucifer is but a servant in my country. A butler or a valet with no power at all. Likes to take credit for my work but he isn't me, and only a dunce would think so. You should die for such a poor answer, though I suppose you tried, so I'll still help you, but only at a steep price.

What price? Mathilde asks.

The Devil whisks out a pair of shears and cuts off all her hair, letting it fall in with the straw.

There, says the Devil, relieved. Now I can work.

While Mathilde sobs into her hands, the Devil sits down before the spinning wheel and whir, whir, whir, three times pulled, the spool is full of gold. Then he puts another one on, and whir, whir, whir, three times pulled, the second is full too. By the time Mathilde is done crying and lifts her head, it is morning and all the straw is spun, and all the spools are gold. The Devil is gone, and in his place stands the king.

Well done, says the king. He makes no mention of her shorn hair or wet cheeks. His eyes are too bright with gold. Come, he says, enjoy some comforts before you're sent home.

Maids flock around Mathilde and spring her off to a hot tub bath, her pick of gowns and jewelry, and a sumptuous feast of Cornish hen, seafood coquille, and chocolate cake. By the end, the miller's daughter is almost smiling. She feels like a princess again. And more important, she's free of the Devil's grasp.

Meanwhile, the red little man watches her in his bubble, as he crouches by his churning river, chuckling to himself.

Lucifer! How predictable. Beautiful girls have no sense. Her next guesses would be even worse. But will there be another turn? That is the question.

He goes to another bubble and checks on the king, who's still marveling at his room piled high with gold. Then the king's eyes turn greedy, twinkling with an idea . . . He bustles out of the room, calling for the maids to bring back the girl.

The Devil laughs.

There is always another turn.

I thought I was going home, says Mathilde.

You are, you are, the king assures. But first, I need you to spin this straw into gold.

Mathilde balks. This room is twice as big—

Naturally. That is the point of a test, says the king. And if you fail it, you will die. Now, now, don't give me that face. What else is a golden goose to do but lay eggs? This is your divine gift, dear girl. And there is no greater honor than to give it to the king. See you in the morning.

He closes the door behind him.

Mathilde looks around the room, crowded floor to ceiling with straw. It is bigger than the house she lives in with her father. She thinks to herself: even the Devil himself couldn't spin so much—

Wrong as usual, says the Devil.

He is there, walking through the door, with his tall black hat and lumpy breeches.

But if I'm to help you, you have to guess my name, and it better be a cleverer guess than yesterday, because I won't take pity on you like I did then.

Mathilde doesn't want to play his games, but at least with a game, she has a chance to win.

Well? says the Devil, tapping his foot. What's my name?

The girl sits taller. Beelzebub, she answers.

The Devil hoots with pleasure. Beelzebub! He

is but a flea on my backside! A wee little vagrant
who prances about Hell like a court jester. He can't
even look in my eyes when we pass! You think the
Devil himself would have a name made from syllables babies babble in their sleep? At least Lucifer
sounded of wickedness and heft, but Beelzebub?
You are a sad, sorry sap, and I should leave you to
die, but I came all this way, so I might as well help
you, though it will cost a dear price.

What price? Mathilde asks.

The Devil thrusts out his claws and turns her
nose, making it humped and crooked.

Much better, he says. Now I can work.

While Mathilde cries over her nose, the Devil sits
down before the spinning wheel and whir, whir, whir,
three times pulled, the spool is full of gold. Then he
puts another one on, and whir, whir, whir, three times
pulled, the second is full too. By the time Mathilde
is done crying and lifts her head, it is morning and
all the straw is spun, and all the spools are gold. The
Devil is gone, and in his place stands the king.

My word! he says, starry-eyed at so much gold,
taking no notice of her nose.

Can I go home now? Mathilde asks, weeping.

Of course, says the king. But don't you want to meet my son, the prince? He should meet a girl of such talents. He is tall and strong and God-fearing, the most eligible bachelor in the land, just returned from battle.

Mathilde stops crying at once. Oh, yes, please—

Maids gaggle in and bustle her away to be bathed and dressed to meet the prince, but when she's brought before him, a man so dashing she can hardly breathe, he takes one look at her scanty hair and crooked nose and sees the mark of the Devil and rides as far from his father's castle as he can.

In his cave, the Devil spies on all this with glee. The prince was an unexpected twist, handsome and holy, but even he wants nothing to do with this blasphemous lot.

There will be no happy ending for Mathilde.

Should have escaped when she had the chance, instead of dilly-dallying for princes.

Now she's fleeing to her carriage, fast as her feet can carry her . . .

Too late.

Palace guards block her way.

The Devil anticipates this, of course.

All good things come in threes.

Lucifer . . . Beelzebub . . . and surely something even more woeful next. Mephistopheles? Leviathan?

So many roads to Hell.

Poor Mathilde. What can she do?

Her soul is evil.

And evil never wins.

This is the biggest room in my castle, says the king, waving his arms around the grand hall. As you can see, every last piece of straw in my kingdom has and there will be time to rest. Humans, on the other hand, have the shortest of life spans and instead of going gently into the night like small, frail leaves on a tree, they insist their short time on earth is only because their souls live eternally and life does not end when they sleep. It is why they arrogantly sail and pollute our seas, laying waste to an earth that does not belong to them. Because they believe themselves superior to the forces that create them. How stupid! How short-sighted! And yet, *you* want to join them, little girl. I find it hard to believe it's all because of one disaster-prone prince, no matter how alluring he might seem. Something else appeals to you about life up there, and I want to know what it is.

Their souls *are* eternal, the mermaid professes. I have proof of it, just like they say. And if I'm part of their world, my soul will live forever with my prince's.

Proof, eh?

As I carried my prince through the storming seas, his eyes opened for the briefest of moments, and in them, I saw purity and goodness beyond what exists in our world. It was like looking through

He doesn't know it was me, says the mermaid. I left him on the beach and watched over him as he slept, until he was found by two girls the next morning.

Were they pretty? the witch asks.

Why does that matter?

Because right now your prince doesn't even know you exist and all the work you did saving him will be attributed to two girls who, from that look on your face, have youth and beauty just like you, but also have springy little legs, which you do not.

That's why I came to you. To make me human, the mermaid says.

Do you know why I am not human even though I could turn myself into one? Because merfolk like you and I live longer. At least three hundred years to a life, which is more than enough time for me to get my fill—right now I'm in a hedonistic phase; a few too many lobster fricassees and caviar compotes—but then there will be new incarnations when I'm done playing the witch . . . a chanteuse . . . a professor . . . a spy named Madame X . . . But when all my reinventions are spent and three hundred years gone, I'll be tired and sated been brought here. If you can spin all this into gold by morning, then there is no test you cannot pass and I will have you as my own wife.

And if I can't? Mathilde asks. She hopes the answer will be: Then I don't want to marry you and you can go home.

But it is not.

Then you will die, of course, says the king.

He hums a tune as he leaves the hall, locking the doors behind him.

A moment later, the doors open and the Devil swaggers in.

Woo-hoo. This is a lot of straw, he says. You will have to make a good guess at my name if I'm to bother helping you.

There's no point, Mathilde laments. If the gold is spun, I have to marry the king and he is a miserly, insatiable ape.

That's the attitude that got you into trouble in the first place, the Devil points out. Only good girls get to marry for love, and you are not good. Besides, with that hair and nose, you'd be lucky to get a rat catcher.

Mathilde blanches. In her mind, she's still beautiful.

The Devil winks. King's too busy counting gold to see what you've become, ha ha.

What you've made me become! Mathilde snaps.

I've only made the outside match the inside, says the Devil.

To this, the girl has no response.

Well? What's my name? the Devil hounds. Answer quick or I'll go find another pretty girl who can't help herself. There's lots, you know.

Mathilde draws a breath. Once upon a time, she was the fairest girl in all the land. Then men began to lay traps for her. Her father. The king. The Devil. Each time, she falls into them, thinking she'll be rescued. That is what storybooks taught her—beauty is goodness, so be beautiful and good things will happen. But it is all lies, and now that she is ugly, she must find a way to save herself.

Azazel, she guesses.

Wrong again! the Devil chimes. So many names you people give me, thinking you can hold me in your head. Name me and I belong to you instead of you to me. But my name is a secret you'll never know and now you have to pay the price if you want my help.

Mathilde gasps. Haven't you done enough to me?

The Devil mulls this over. Okay, if that's the way you want to play it. Fine. I won't hurt you. But if I spin this straw into gold, then I will take your firstborn child, and I'll do whatever I want with it. Promise?

Mathilde balks. Like her mother and father, she is marked for the Devil's hands. And now he wants to mark the next in line. There is no goodness in the Devil to appeal to. No compassion or mercy or boundaries. He will take and take until there is nothing but pain. She must break the chain. She must find her own goodness. The kind of goodness that can summon angels. The kind of goodness that will save her future child from joining her in Hell. And to do that, she must live another day.

Promise, she says.

The Devil slashes a mark into her hand, a reminder of their deal. Then he spins and spins until morning's light.

When the king comes, he finds a grand hall filled with gold, just as he asked, and days later, he marries Mathilde in an extravagant wedding, and the miller's daughter becomes queen.

A year later, the queen brings a baby boy into the world. It is the first time she's ever felt love in her life. But with love comes fear. Each night, she clutches her son as she sleeps, afraid the Devil will take him. But he doesn't show, and soon she sleeps easier and easier, her grip softening, until she forgets about the Devil completely—

That's when he appears.

It is the middle of the night, and he startles her from sleep.

Go away! she shouts, holding her son close.

Forgive me, Your Highness. What's that I see on the back of your hand? the Devil says. Might it be . . . the mark of a *promise*?

The queen bolts to the door to call her guards, but the Devil sweeps the rug from under her, sending the queen crashing to the ground and the child flying out of her arms into the Devil's grasp. His claws curl over the little boy's mouth, snuffing his cries.

Please, Mathilde sobs. I'll give you all the wealth in our kingdom . . . anything you want . . .

What do I need with treasure, the Devil laughs,

pinching the boy's ears. I'll have more fun with this one.

There must be something else! Mathilde begs.

The Devil considers this. One game has already yielded two souls. A happy bonus. And yet, the best things come in threes. . . .

All right, then, he says. I'll give you three days to guess my name. No leeway this time. Only the right name will win. If by the end of three days, you know my name, then you may have your child back. But if you don't, then I will take your next child too.

With that, he blows the queen a kiss and spirits her son away.

◦✕◦

Mathilde rushes to the king.

Their son is missing. The Devil has taken him and to get him back, they must learn the Devil's name.

The king is used to giving tests, not passing them, so he tells her this is her problem to solve, and if she does not retrieve their son in three days' time, then she will lose her head as punishment. There are plenty of other queens he can marry who won't have the Devil haunting his court.

Mathilde runs to the palace guards for help, but they want nothing to do with the Devil. Nor do the maids or the cooks. She even goes to her father, but the king has sent the miller to find new brides should the queen have to die, and naturally her father obliges, since the mission is well paid.

So it is up to Mathilde now.

There is no man to rescue her like in fairy tales.

If she's to beat the Devil, she must be her own prince.

The first day, she disguises herself as a peasant and visits all the markets in the kingdom, chumming up to shopkeepers and patrons and homeless vagabonds in alleys, asking if anyone knows the Devil's name. This frightens away most souls, but a few have their ideas, and she writes them down, hoping one is the answer she is looking for.

At night, the Devil comes, clutching her son as his own, and she is ready.

Is it Tchort? Rimmon? Moloch? Dracul? she asks.

Wrong, wrong, wrong, he says. Two more days!

He vanishes into the dark.

Mathilde grits her teeth.

She will not give up.

The second day, the queen again disguises herself and travels to the outskirts of the kingdom, where clans live in the darkest parts of the forest, out of reach of the king. She asks them if they know the name of the Devil, and here they are not so afraid of speaking their mind, so they tell her what they know, and she writes it down.

At night, the Devil comes with her child and she is ready.

Chemosh? Hecate? Baphomet? Nihasa? Mastema? she asks.

Wrong, wrong, wrong, he says. One more day!

He vanishes into the dark.

Mathilde can't sleep. She takes a horse and rides into the mountains, where no one can find her. There she sits as the sun rises, thinking of the moments in her life when she went wrong, the forks in the road where she took the false path, and she asks her angels to give her a way back. Silence yawns. No answer comes. Soon it is nightfall and it's time to face the Devil one last time. But as she returns through the woods, a wildfire sparks, leaping over trees, chasing toward her. More proof her soul is marked. She rides away, but the flames grasp for her like long, twisted talons, trapping her and her horse in a cursed circle. She won't get to kiss her son again. She won't get to say goodbye. In the last moments before she burns, she wishes she could take her boy's place in the Devil's hands, that she could free his soul and steal his pain. Fire leaps at her like a noose—

Then a cool rain.

She looks into the sky as flames die.

Rain fills her eye before it spills down her cheeks.

A last mercy.

In the bedroom, she waits for the Devil.

He comes on time, Mathilde's son whimpering in his grip.

One more chance, he says. What's my name?

Before I guess, the queen says, may I hold him and say goodbye?

The Devil can't resist suffering.

He gives the boy to the queen, and she brings him to her breast. His cries go quiet, his tiny fingers wrapped in hers. Mathilde's tears sparkle on his head like a cool rain. Gently she kisses him and blesses him with the strength to endure, the courage to be good, the grace of better angels.

In return, he babbles softly into her ear, the syllables only a baby knows, that together have the rhythm of a name.

It's time, the Devil says.

Claws out, he swoops for his spawn—

Rumpel . . . stilt . . . skin, Mathilde says.

The Devil freezes in his tracks.

The queen looks at him.

That's your name, isn't it?

Rumpelstiltskin.

A tail bursts free from his pants. His horns cut sharper. The redness swells in his cheeks as if he might swallow her whole.

The Devil points at the child. He told you that! He told you that!

But a deal is a deal.

Mathilde keeps her boy.

The little red man stomps his right foot so hard it breaks the floor, and he falls in to his waist. He can't get back out, no matter how hard he tries. He looks to the queen to save him. She doesn't. The Devil has a name now. A beginning and an end. He curses Mathilde, again and again, just words, just sounds, until all that comes out of his mouth is spittle and smoke. With both hands he flails at his foot, unable to dig out of the hole he's made for himself, so he whips his tail, lashing himself with awful shouts, turning redder, redder, before he takes hold of his other leg and rips himself up the middle, right in two.

By the time the guards come running, all that remains is his ragged little breeches, the kind that might be strewn about by a child.

Her hair lengthens, her nose smooths back, her child grows big and strong, handsomer than any prince, nourished by her love. Love that surprises

her with its force. Love that is selfless, bottomless, the true measure of her soul.

As for the king, he goes hunting one day with the girl's father and something goes wrong, for both men are recovered crushed beneath a tree.

An accident, everyone says.

On Sundays thereafter, the queen visits their graves.

But the Sunday before Christmas, her father and husband are missing from the places they were laid.

All that's left are big, black holes, as if something reached out from the deepest part of the earth and dragged them both in.

DEAR YOU,

Sing a song of love.

That's what my mother used to tell me whenever I felt down in those first days after Neverland.

Sing a song of love and your spirit will lift.

Perhaps she knew I was in love with Peter Pan before I did.

I was only twelve when Peter swept me away to that world beyond the clouds, past the North Star, an archipelago of islands that every child knows in their bones. Pirates, mermaids, fairies, warrior clans, wild beasts . . . All stake their claim, brought to life by children who believe in them, for young dreams are the fuel of Neverland, and its splashes of color so bright and startling you can't find them anywhere on earth. Neverland is ever-changing, islands lost and islands added, depending on what young souls are dreaming about, because children tend to converge on the same dreams, even if they live on opposite sides of the sun. Last I heard, the fairies have lost territory to giant bugs; the pirate island grows bigger, encroaching on the mermaid lagoon; and the warrior clans have been replaced by man-eating dinosaurs. But even more peculiar are the changes in Neverland that *I* am responsible for: the new species of great white bird called a *Wendy*, the giant sewing thimbles that mysteriously wash upon the shores, the young girls who wander onto the island looking for lost boys to mother . . . You see, the story of my time in Neverland has become famous, a fairy tale every child learns growing up. So now children dream about me and my marvelous adventures, and they do it with such force and communion that the story of Peter Pan and Wendy in Neverland has become a part of Neverland itself.

Like all fairy tales though, that one had an end. As the story goes, Peter Pan brought me and my brothers, Michael and John, back home to Bloomsbury, where the wind blows cold and the skies fog gray, and we grew up into the usual stale old adults, losing grip on our memories of Peter and Neverland with each passing year.

But that's not the true end to the tale.

No one knows that, except me and . . .

Well, let me start from the beginning. The beginning of the end.

I was always meant to be a mother. Anyone could have told you that. Bossing Michael and John around from the moment they popped out, acting as if they were my sole responsibility—brush your teeth! eat your squash! put your shoes away! I hounded—and while Mother found all this tedious, I could hear Father in the corner, as he counted his shillings, mumbling: She'll make a good wife someday!

No wonder Peter chose my window to alight. I saw a handsome boy come to be my prince, and he saw a governess for lost boys, who could herd spirits and mend underpants. What else is a girl good for? This was the paradox we could never undo: that I wanted Peter's love, while he wanted my labor. Is it any surprise he confused kisses for thimbles?

The more I loved Peter, the worse things got (the first sign of a doomed relationship). Pirates kidnapped me, lost boys shot me with arrows, Peter's fairy, Tinker Bell, seethed with jealousy and plotted my demise. . . . A girl can only take so much before it's time to go home. There would be no Wendy and Peter. My first heartbreak. My first poisonous taste of adulthood. Back at the house, I slunk around like a prickly cat, obsessively tidying cupboards, sewing socks we didn't need, hissing at my brothers to pick up their toys and stop peeking longingly at clouds. Sing a song of love, my mother gently encouraged me. But love was a fairy tale, and I'd grown too old for those.

Peter wasn't done with me though. He came in the middle of the night to kidnap me again—the lost boys missed their Wendy and he'd promised to get me back—but I screamed in surprise, and Mother came running and she lashed Peter to the bedpost and chastised him like he was her son. In the end, he and Mother agreed to a deal: that I would fly one week a year to Neverland at the top of spring to do his and the boys' cleaning. As my mother put it, she didn't have much choice. Peter was a little terrorist, and she'd rather have an appointed week for kidnapping than fret losing me each and every night. But I also suspect she saw the fresh spark in my eyes and heard the songs I hummed in the days that followed, songs of love about a boy I couldn't quit, and Mother realized that losing me one week a year was the price to have me happy for all the rest.

The first few trips back to Neverland were glorious. Peter knew he only had me for seven days each time, so he whisked me along and incited needless commotion, insistent that we find big adventures. There was the year he stole the mermaids' prized black pearl for me, which left us imprisoned in the sea king's brig, before I charmed a family of seahorses into bailing us out. There was the year Peter brewed a witch's recipe, thinking he could turn back time so we'd have more days together, only to shrink us both to the size of newts. Then the year Peter fed me Giggly Wigglies, little fluorescing forest worms that make you laugh so hard you can't stop, and we awakened all the wild beasts, which chased us across land and sea. Still, no matter the danger, every adventure ended with Peter rescuing me or me rescuing Peter, and a race to get to the North Star and rush me home before the end of the seventh day, with a flurry of memories to last until next spring.

Then came the year I turned sixteen and everything changed.

Peter brought me to Neverland at the appointed time, but now he scowled at me with disgust. You've grown old, he said. There was no greater offense to Peter than growing old. Indeed, any lost boy who woke one morning with hair on his chin or a smattering of pimples or a changed voice would soon vanish from sight—Peter called it 'thinning out the herd,' the law of nature, but we all knew he killed the boys himself. Now he looked upon my blooming body with the same murderous eye, as if he might kill me too if I wasn't due back to my parents in such a short while. This time, when pirates kidnapped me, as pirates often did, Peter didn't care.

Captain Hook was dead by then, Peter Pan having fed him to a crocodile. Only three pirates in the crew had survived the final battle between Peter and Hook—Smee, the Irish bosun; Gentleman Starkey, who'd been kidnapped by island clans; and Scourie, first lieutenant—so Smee recruited a new gang of handsome brutes with cropped hair and angry faces who reminded me of the boys back in England returning from war. Smee's pirates tied me to the mast, expecting Peter to save me, whereby they'd launch into battle, and there I stayed for two days, with Smee scratching his bald little head while peering out his periscope because Peter never came.

Now you must be feeling sorry for me, bound to a pole on an enemy vessel for such a long time, imagining I was racked with pain and fear, especially with Scourie guarding me. Scourie was Captain Hook's most trusted henchman, the one who had the deepest disdain for Peter, so naturally they put me in his hands, knowing there'd be no funny business. He was a scary-looking lad, eighteen years old, with pale pink skin, heavy-lidded eyes, a bumpy nose, and stubbled cheeks. For the first day, he stood there, leaning against the ship rail, staring at me for hours straight, like he could see inside me, never once looking away, those dark eyes sizzling like coals. Then when everyone went to sleep, he glanced around to make sure the deck was clear before he ripped his sword off his belt and came toward me, like he would chop me in two.

Instead, he cut me loose.

Sit down, he said.

I obeyed, less because of his order and more because my legs were throbbing. The ship was anchored close to shore, so close that swampy man-grove trees shaded the deck with their branches, through which I could see the black of night and bright stars winking at me, like I was right where I should be.

Scourie shoved a jug of water at me and a biscuit with salted beef.

Must be tired, he growled. Get some grub in your stomach and then put yourself to sleep. I'll watch over ya.

You're not my mother. Don't tell me what to do,

I snapped. I get enough of that from Peter.

Peter is a dastardly fella leaving you here like this, he said. Not surprising though. Thinks of nothing but himself.

Much as I wanted to argue, I couldn't, because it was true.

I noticed he didn't talk like the other pirates who gnarred and garbled their words; Scourie's tone was smooth and crisp, his vowels articulate. There was no doubt he'd been to school.

How did you come to be on a pirate ship? I asked.

Same way you came to be the wench of a git like Peter: it's my lot in life, Scourie retorted. He must have seen my frown, because he sighed and sat down across from me. Want my story, then? Fine. Born in a hell called Bloodbrook with a nasty father and ran away when I was ten. Sheriff found me and dumped me in an orphanage, where I was sold to the headmistress of Blackpool, a fine institution that breeds pirates to sail the savage seas. Best lads got sent to the *Jolly Roger*, the ship of Captain James Hook, because Hook was a man of education and refinement and wanted the best of Blackpool's lot. So I buckled down and studied best I could—geography, mathematics, astronomy, history, as well as nautical arts and maritime law—and lo and behold, I got called up to the *Roger* at the ripe age of twelve, since Hook went through ten men a month, either because he killed them when they put a foot wrong or because they were dispatched by Peter Pan during his and Hook's weekly battles. I was the lowest rank when I joined, but I lived longer than most and rose quickly to become Hook's best lieutenant. They say he's dead, but that's a load of dung if you ask me, since Hook's died many times before and always finds his way back. His blood isn't like yours or mine, you know; it's a strange color, like he's made of the devil. But for now, Hook's gone and Smee ain't much of a captain, so we're less well-oiled pirate crew and more bored old bunch, hunting for trouble just so we can be less bored. Truth is, I wonder if I've outgrown it all, the way you have.

I don't think I'll ever outgrow Neverland, I countered.

Sure you will, he replied. You already have. Why do you think Peter doesn't want you anymore? Because he knows the times a-comin' when you'll find true love with some dullard from your world who wears nice clothes and tends to a bank and you'll forget this place ever existed.

The words about Peter stung. I sat taller, returning his glare. And what if my true love is *in* Neverland? Then it's only a matter of time before he sees I'm the one he's meant to be with. Then I'll stay here forever.

Peter, you mean? Peter Pan, your true love? Scourie chuckled. Barking up the wrong tree with that one. Look what Tinker Bell's become, trying to win his heart. Once a bright fairy. Now a bitter little mongrel. She should know better by now. So should you. Only person Peter could ever love is Peter.

He pointed at the biscuit. Not hungry?

I didn't answer.

Here then, he said.

He drew something out of his pocket.

A blue flower, the leafy calyx enclosing a shimmering blue fruit.

Mermaid's Delight, said Scourie. Blooms only one day a year from an underwater tree and tastes so good you'll feel things in your heart you never knew you could. We stole one on our last raid. Supposed to keep it for the first pirate that strikes Peter a blow when he rescues you, but since that's not gonna happen . . .

I gazed at the succulent fruit, my mouth growing wet.

You'd give it to me? I asked.

Scourie smiled. If you promise we'll meet again.

My eyes lifted to his, surprised.

An arrow stabbed his bicep—

Whooping lost boys swung onto the ship, led by

their cocky young leader in a tunic made of leaves, waking all the pirates, who stormed on deck in their pajamas.

Peter, like the pirates, had grown bored too.

I don't remember much of what happened after that. Peter flew me away from the *Jolly Roger*, and I spent the remainder of the week playing mother to his lost boys, with Peter showing little interest in me, and when the seventh day was over, I returned through the North Star, to family, school, and life.

The next spring, Peter didn't come.

And the strange part was . . . I didn't mind. I'd seen now what Peter Pan was. A boy who would never grow up. Perhaps Scourie was right. One day, true love would be found in a Bloomsbury bloke who wore a tie and didn't know how to fly. It was time to let go of Neverland.

But then a night that spring, an odd glow hit my window. Neither Michael nor John stirred, but I snuck from my bed and pressed my face to the glass, the glittery light growing stronger and stronger—

A ladder dropped into view.

I lifted the window and looked into the sky at

the *Jolly Roger*, floating overhead in a cloud of fairy dust, the ladder unspooled from its deck. Scourie loomed at the top, his eyes gleaming like the stars around him.

When I climbed to the top, he had a familiar blue fruit in hand.

You forgot this, he said.

Kept it for me a whole year? I asked.

Don't be a goose. Mermaid's Delight goes bad like everything else. So I went down to the bottom of the ocean and got you another one. Then had to steal enough fairy dust to fly the ship here. Lot of work you are.

I looked at Scourie. For once his clothes weren't filthy, and he wore a brown velvet vest, like he'd dressed up for the occasion. His face was smooth, his pants belted, and his shirt tucked in. He smelled nice too, like honey and spice.

He held out the little blue orb. Here, he said. Don't make me have come all this way for nothin'.

I reached out and took it from him, the soft blue skin like fresh suede.

Close your eyes, he said. Take a bite.

I obeyed.

There's no words for how it tasted, but let me try. It's at once tart and minty, warm and nutty, and wet and thick, like you've bit into a blue forest. The flavor is so rich, so unfamiliar, that your breath falls out of you and your heart skips faster, like all your faculties are not enough and your mind and body must expand to new sensations. Inside yourself, you feel dimensions you never thought possible, as if you're more than what you think and you're as infinite as possibility, until you flare open your eyes just in time to remember . . . that there is a person who gifted this moment, a pirate in moonlight, and in his eyes, I can see to the end of the universe. But then the taste slides away and it's gone, leaving only a residue, a heightened awareness of everything around—including the fact there is no one else on this ship.

Wait. Where *is* everyone? I asked.

Because as far as I could tell, the *Jolly Roger* was empty, save its first lieutenant and me.

Oh, they're all off fighting the clans, said Scourie. Told them I'd man the ship offshore. They'll be busy chasing tail till dawn.

That night, as the *Roger* hid in the clouds over

Bloomsbury, Scourie and I sat on a hammock he threaded between stars and drank bubbly peach cider he'd made himself.

Is your world any fun at all? he asked, peering down at the rows of night-lit houses. From up here, everything looks so . . . boxy.

Fun can be overrated, I replied. Too much of it and then it doesn't mean very much. Like living on candy instead of saving it for special occasions. That's what Nana says, at least. Or I think it's what she says. Dogs can be obtuse sometimes.

Who's Nana? he asked.

Our nurse. I know it doesn't make much sense having a dog as a nurse—

Of course it does. What better nurse can there be than a dog?

He grinned, as if to remind me there were no rules in the world he came from. And yet, all I could think of were the rules I was breaking. I was a traitor to Peter being here. In Captain Hook's ship! With Captain Hook's pirate! I knew I should feel guilty. Peter was my first love and Scourie his enemy. But how can you feel guilty when you're having such a good time?

You're right, I sighed. My world is very boxy.

His hand brushed mine, and for a moment, I thought it an accident until he left it there, our fingers touching.

Peter told us you give him kisses, Scourie said.

I turned to him sharply.

When my pirates and I captured him, he added. Bragged he'd gotten a girl's kisses and when we asked whose, Peter showed us your sewing thimble that he wears around his neck. . . . Said it's the best kiss he's ever gotten.

Scourie looked at me. We burst into laughter.

He doesn't understand, I said.

I do, said Scourie.

The night clung to his words. How quiet everything became.

But Scourie said nothing else, made no further move.

How do you ask a boy to kiss you? How do you tell him it's okay?

By the time I found the courage, it was too late.

Dawn raided the darkness. Time to go home.

Only I wasn't ready to say goodbye.

Come back for me, I said. First night of spring.

My mother will think you're Peter. We'll have a week. You and I.

I expected Scourie to agree at once, to smile and hug me into his chest. But instead he frowned, pensive and grim.

And what of all the other weeks? he asked.

The question echoed in my heart, summer, fall, winter, until the very last seeds of snow shrunk into the soil. All the while, a strange heat stoked inside me, like all my senses had caught fire, making colors sharper, smells and tastes crisper, the humdrum life of Bloomsbury suddenly alive. With Peter, it had been butterflies in my stomach, the sick feeling of grasping onto love unrequited, but this was different. This was a low and steady roar, like my soul had found its match and now was on the hunt for reunion.

On the first night of spring, I didn't sleep, waiting for the glow of fairy dust to light my window, and when it came, I bounded to the glass and threw it open—

Peter stared back at me.

It's Tink, he said. She's dying.

All thoughts of Scourie were buried. I had just

enough time to sneak downstairs and pack a bag full of medicines before Peter sprinkled me with the fairy dust he had left and flew me back to Neverland. Deep in the forest, the lost boys bowed their heads, watching Tinker Bell gasp for breath, as she lay shriveled and dim on a tree stump.

What's happened? I asked.

Mushrooms, said a boy. She found glowing ones in the wildebeest fields and wanted to give them to Peter as a gift, so she tasted one to make sure they were safe. . . .

Peter lowered his head. Poor Tink, he said.

She's poisoned, then! I cried.

Instantly, I drew my bag of medicines. Michael had once inhaled a pinch of rat poison, thinking it was sugar, and I remember all that Mother had done. Two charcoal tablets and a teaspoon of castor oil—

I pried open Tink's tiny mouth and tipped the black powder under her tongue along with oily liquid from a vial . . .

By morning, Tink was snoozing comfortably in Peter's lap, the poison expelled, and Peter stroked her hair with his thumbs.

Tink, wasn't I clever to call Wendy? Peter said, glancing up at me. Maybe I should marry Wendy so she can't ever leave again. Then I'd have to grow up, wouldn't I? But we'd have our Wendy, and we'd all be safe and loved forever. . . .

Words that once would have rang the bells of my heart now landed with a hollow thud.

And indeed, he kept his eyes well on me in the days that followed, hovering possessively in a way he never had before, perhaps sensing my gaze always roving toward the outlines of the *Jolly Roger*, hiding in sea mist beyond the forest. Finally, on the third night, once he and the boys were asleep, I snuck away, padding through trees, wading through swamps to get to the coastline, then swimming into balmy waters, out toward Captain Hook's ship. I grabbed hold of one of the cannons and wedged myself up, climbing the portholes until I made it to the ship rail, about to slide over the edge onto deck—

Burlap dunked over my head, bagging me up.

I kicked and squirmed, shouting for my life, before I felt the sack dropped onto hard floor . . . then an undulation of waves and the sound of oars in water, like I was being taken out into the ocean to be drowned. I was so scared I could feel myself detaching from my own body, like I was practicing how to die—

Then the sack opened.

Scourie glared down at me. He loomed tall in a rowboat, framed by the mangroves of the swamp.

Thought we had an appointment at your window, he said coldly. First night of spring.

Yes, I rasped. But—

He grabbed my wrist. I saw you go with Peter instead, he snarled. Is that why you're sneaking onto my ship? Was all this part of his plan? You still his wench?

No! I said. No.

Scourie's eyes flayed me like they did that first night he was on guard. How do I know you're not lying? he demanded.

Because Peter would kill me if he knew I was here, I answered.

Scourie stared at me a long while.

He let go of my hand.

Lot of work you are, he growled. Lot of work.

He stepped off the boat, tramping into the swamp.

Then he glanced back with a surly grin.

Well? What you waiting for now?

That night and in the nights that followed, Scourie was my guide. During the day, I'd nest with Peter and the boys, finding spare moments to nap, before absconding in darkness to the swamps where my pirate would be waiting. Then, like two shadows, we'd slip away to sights of Neverland I'd never seen. The ghost ship armada . . . the waterfall of wishes . . . the unicorn mountains . . . But it was the butterfly caves that I remember most, because it was where Scourie and I huddled side by side, close in the darkness, sharing bread dipped in chocolate and watching luminous wings dive and dance around us. A blue butterfly landed on my nose, and I peeked over, expecting him to laugh. Instead, I saw a tear in his eye.

I thought pirates were bloodthirsty goons who drank the blood of men, I said. And here you are, brought to heel by a butterfly.

He shook his head. No, it's just . . . I've long dreamed of bringing someone here. But villains can't have love. That's what I was taught.

You're not a villain— I started.

He turned to me, and his face hardened to stone.
I saw the pirate he was.

Yes, I am, he said. And if Smee or any of the
others knew I was here with you, they'd mount my
head on a pike.

Then why be a pirate at all? I pushed, unafraid.
Why not choose another life?

Because a pirate's life is the closest thing to glory,
he said. To be a pirate is to rise from nothing and
fight to have your name remembered. That's what
all of us want. To have a legacy that outlives us. To
have our name in storybooks.

That's glory? I scoffed. To have people you'll
never meet know your name?

Well, some like Hook want every soul in heaven
and earth to revere their name, he said. I just want
one. One person who will hold my name in their
heart.

You already have that, I said. Scourie of Bloodbrook.

His eyes met mine.

Who made you, he breathed. Who made someone so wondrous and pure?

I fidgeted. Peter says I'm a fussy old nag who

doesn't know how to have fun—

Peter is a good-for-nothing ass, he said.

I wrung my hands harder. Well, you don't really know me yet.

I don't? He chuckled. Then let me tell you what I do know about you. The way the freckles on your nose light up in sun. The way you lean on your right foot when you're thinking. The way you eat a piece of fruit with two hands instead of one. The way you look away when I say anything nice about you. The way you sit stiff when I say something boorish or rude. The way you look at me like no one has ever looked at me, like I'm a human, like I have a heart. The way you are, Wendy. I love you for all of it. So tell me now I don't know you.

I couldn't speak.

Scourie's eyes glittered like fire. If you won't say anything, then maybe you'll give me a thimble instead?

Our lips touched.

My first real kiss.

With a pirate instead of a Pan.

When our mouths parted, we held each other in the glow of a thousand wings.

But then rose a strange light strobing faster, brighter than the rest, blinding us both before it went dark and disappeared.

I gripped Scourie's hand.

Tinker Bell.

She'd seen us.

Scourie tried to stop me, but I was already running, out of the caves, down the mountain, into the forest, back from where Tinker Bell came.

By the time I arrived, Peter had condemned me to die.

Wait! I choked—but ten of his boys rushed in and bound me to a tree, the same way Hook's pirates once lashed me to their mast.

Peter brandished a dagger, prowling toward me, his grin wicked and vengeful, as if he would take as much pleasure casting me out of his world as he did bringing me in. Tinker Bell hovered on his shoulder, leering at me—me, who'd saved her life—but Peter's musings about marrying me had roused her jealousy and sealed my fate.

Peter, listen to me, I started. You didn't want me. You didn't even come last year. That's why I—

Kissing pirates, he sneered. I'd say that's a crime worthy of death!

Aye! the boys chorused.

Sneaking out after dark, added Peter. That's a crime worthy of death!

Aye! said the boys.

Pretending to care about us when she was a pirate's wench. A crime worthy of death!

Aye!

And growing up into a dirty, lying traitor, Peter resounded. That's the worst crime of all!

Aye!

For all those things and more, I sentence Wendy to die! Peter roared.

Aye! Aye! Aye!

As Peter came toward me, his knife shined in Tinker Bell's glow and his boys whooped a chant—*Kill the Wendy! Booga-loo! Kill the Wendy! Booga-loo!*—while they hopped from foot to foot and wagged their bums, like a flock of savage birds.

Peter drew closer. You know where traitors go, Wendy? Same place Hook went. Say hello to the old chap, will you?

He raised the knife and a red spot lit up in each

eye, like a demon within. Then he plunged the blade at my breast—

A shadow bomb fell from the tree, smashing Peter in the head. Peter staggered up, waving his knife blindly, but Scourie was on him, slapping the boy so hard he spun to the ground, losing two baby teeth in the process. In a flash, Peter's gang flew at Scourie, but they were boys and Scourie almost a man, and he whipped off his belt and swung it at any who got close, thrashing them until he could get to me on the tree and rip me loose—

Tinker Bell bashed him from behind, biting Scourie's neck like a bat and drawing blood, clawing at his eyes to scratch them out, until I lunged and caught her in my fist.

You bitter . . . little . . . mongrel, I hissed, shaking her by her bottom, spilling gold dust out of her before throwing her into the bushes.

Meanwhile, Peter and the boys were back on their feet, hacking at us with spears and swords and everything they had—

But Scourie and I were already off ground, lifting into the night, haloed in Tink's dust.

Scourie glowered down at Peter. Come anywhere

near Wendy and I'll drink your blood for supper, he snarled.

He gave me a little wink.

Then we shot out of Neverland like bats out of hell, back to the world of banks and blokes and other boxy things.

Naturally, Peter came to kill me, but Scourie was there each night, guarding my window while my brothers and I slept, and he pummeled Peter so many times that Peter stopped trying, as sore losers often do. Still, he had one last revenge: tattling to Smee and his pirates that Scourie had been sneaking off with Peter's lass, which led to Scourie getting a vicious flogging and a promise of sure death if he ever saw Wendy again. But as soon as Scourie could get away, he did, lighting up my window, armed with the stolen dust of fairies, ready to fly me into the sky. Some weeks he came every night, some months he didn't come at all; I never asked what kept him, instead savoring our moments, thankful he'd crossed between worlds one more time.

Years passed, and I was a woman now. Scourie's visits grew more infrequent—Smee's eyes were

on him, he'd say to me . . . hard to get away . . .
fairies were watching for him. . . . In time, I married, a man named Harry who worked at a bank
and called me pumpkin and went to bed at nine
thirty sharp and got up at six, but still Scourie came
when he could, flying me away while my husband
snored soundly in our bed. I told myself I should
put an end to it, that I should bar my window, bolt
the shutters, lock Scourie out. . . . But how could
I? It never felt wrong with Scourie, just as it never
felt wrong when we roamed Neverland while Peter
slept. Of course I wished that he and I could be
together always, that it should have been Scourie
who married me, but to what end? He was a pirate
of Neverland, and I was a girl of the mundane. To
be together, we would have to live somewhere in the
middle, and no middle exists between the fantasy
and the real. So I lived two lives, one by day, one on
those luckiest of nights, and I searched for guilt in
the wake of this deception, only to find gratitude
instead—that I had this gift of love in the form of
a man, come to wake my soul, whenever it was in
danger of entombing in sleep.

Harry suspected nothing, of course. He had his

money to count, his dinner on the table at six, his whiskey at eight, and soon, a child to look forward to. If asked, I'm sure he would say he loved me, as I would say I loved him, but neither of us asked, and so the words were never spoken. We were each a means to an end. He wasn't even there when I went into labor, having departed for a meeting in Moscow.

Oh dear, came early, did it? he sighed over the phone. I won't get back in time, pumpkin. Wishing you the best.

When my baby was born, he came out limp.

He had pink pale skin and his eyes were closed, his tiny hands shaky, the life gone before it came.

The doctor said he had a weak heart (bad luck, nothing to be done) and left me alone with my new-born son, in a dim, sour-smelling room.

I held him to my chest, a small, feeble body, my heart trying to pump health into his. He was my child. I'd find a way to make him strong . . . to make him happy . . . Yet, with each second, his heartbeat grew fainter, his breaths softer—

Then a light touched the window, a warm, golden glow expanding against frosted glass, and when I pulled it open, Scourie floated through.

Without a word, he took his son and wrapped his naked little body in frog pajamas, before he put his mouth to the child's and breathed deep into him. My baby boy choked and let out a bold, effortful cry, his big black eyes flying open to the antiseptic room. He whimpered and coughed, his hands flailing as if to peel away the air.

This world isn't for him. That's why he's weak, Scourie said. His soul lives in Neverland.

He swaddled the boy in his pajamas, sprinkling him with fairy dust before showering me with the last of it. Come, Wendy. We must take him home before it's too late.

The child in his arms, Scourie lofted toward the window, then glimpsed my shadow on the wall, unmoving behind him. He spun around—

Fly, Wendy! Fly now!

I can't, I rasped.

And it was true.

I could no longer fly, the fairy dust turned to ash on my skin.

Voices rose down the hall. They'd heard the boy's cry.

Scourie rushed to me, struggling to hoist me up and carry me too.

But it couldn't be done.

Try again . . . , Scourie pleaded with me. Try harder!

But the harder I tried, the more rooted I stayed.

My son's birth was the last bit of magic my body could take. I'd grown up once and for all. I couldn't live between worlds any longer.

Take him with you, I wept.

No . . . he's your child . . . Scourie held him out to me. I can't keep him from you—

He's *our* child. And our child must be happy, I said, my voice gaining strength. He can't thrive here. This world is choking him. This world that closes off possibilities, when he deserves them all.

Scourie shook his head, but I gripped my pirate close.

Take him, I begged. Take our son where he belongs and teach him he was loved. Teach him he was *made* by love.

Scourie's tears fell on my face. He kissed me, again and again. Always, he said. Always. I'll come back for you. I will. We'll be together one day. We'll be a family. You'll see—

But our boy was wheezing now, strangled for air, with nurses knocking on my door. Scourie gave me one last kiss. Then he held our son to his heart and soared out the window into the chilled night air, and I heard my child gasp full, beautiful breaths as he flew toward where he belonged.

Scourie never came back.

He couldn't.

My portal to Neverland had closed, the North

Star gone dark, my bridge to the world of dreams broken.

Now I write this letter to you before I set it free to the sea, hoping that one day, by any magic left in me, my words find you, wherever you are. For you are in my heart always, both the pain of knowing I cannot watch you grow up and the joy of knowing you have a father who brought you to life, like he once did to me. But now you'll know you have a mother too. You'll know her name is Wendy and she lives in a world far away from your own. And even if she isn't there at your side, even if she isn't there to kiss and hold you, you'll know she's been there all along, telling this story to herself to keep herself whole, so that one day she could tell it to you.

You, my baby boy in frog pajamas, who are loved, loved, loved, and I sing a song each night in your name.

Your mother,
Wendy

Read the beginning of
Soman Chainani's bestselling series
THE SCHOOL FOR GOOD AND EVIL

1

The Princess & The Witch

Sophie had waited all her life to be kidnapped.
But tonight, all the other children
of Gavaldon writhed in their beds.
If the School Master took them,
they'd never return. Never lead
a full life. Never see their family again.
Tonight these children dreamt of a red-
eyed thief with the body of a beast, come
to rip them from their
sheets and stifle their
screams.

Sophie dreamt
of princes instead.

She had arrived
at a castle ball
thrown in her

honor, only to find the hall filled with a hundred suitors and no other girls in sight. Here for the first time were boys who deserved her, she thought as she walked the line. Hair shiny and thick, muscles taut through shirts, skin smooth and tan, beautiful and attentive like princes should be. But just as she came to one who seemed better than the rest, with brilliant blue eyes and ghostly white hair, the one who felt like Happily Ever After . . . a hammer broke through the walls of the room and smashed the princes to shards.

Sophie's eyes opened to morning. The hammer was real. The princes were not.

"Father, if I don't sleep nine hours, my eyes look swollen."

"Everyone's prattling on that you're to be taken this year," her father said, nailing a misshapen bar over her bedroom window, now completely obscured by locks, spikes, and screws. "They tell me to shear your hair, muddy up your face, as if I believe all this fairy-tale hogwash. But no one's getting in here tonight. That's for sure." He pounded a deafening crack as exclamation.

Sophie rubbed her ears and frowned at her once lovely window, now something you'd see in a witch's den. "Locks. Why didn't anyone think of that before?"

"I don't know why they all think it's you," he said, silver hair slicked with sweat. "If it's goodness that School Master fellow wants, he'll take Gunilda's daughter."

Sophie tensed. "Belle?"

"Perfect child that one is," he said. "Brings her father home-cooked lunches at the mill. Gives the leftovers to the poor hag in the square."

Sophie heard the edge in her father's voice. She had never once cooked a full meal for him, even after her mother died. Naturally she had good reason (the oil and smoke would clog her pores) but she knew it was a sore point. This didn't mean her father had gone hungry. Instead, she offered him her own favorite foods: mashed beets, broccoli stew, boiled asparagus, steamed spinach. He hadn't ballooned into a blimp like Belle's father, precisely because she hadn't brought him home-cooked lamb fricassees and cheese soufflés at the mill. As for the poor hag in the square, that old crone, despite claiming hunger day after day, was *fat*. And if Belle had anything to do with it, then she wasn't good at all, but the worst kind of evil.

Sophie smiled back at her father. "Like you said, it's all hog-wash." She swept out of bed and slammed the bathroom door.

She studied her face in the mirror. The rude awakening had taken its toll. Her waist-long hair, the color of spun gold, didn't have its usual sheen. Her jade-green eyes looked faded, her lus-cious red lips a touch dry. Even the glow of her creamy peach skin had dulled. *But still a princess*, she thought. Her father couldn't see she was special, but her mother had. "You are too beautiful for this world, Sophie," she said with her last breaths. Her mother had gone somewhere better and now so would she.

Tonight she would be taken into the woods. Tonight she would begin a new life. Tonight she would live out her fairy tale.

And now she needed to look the part.

To begin, she rubbed fish eggs into her skin, which smelled

of dirty feet but warded off spots. Then she massaged in pumpkin puree, rinsed with goat's milk, and soaked her face in a mask of melon and turtle egg yolk. As she waited for the mask to dry, Sophie flipped through a storybook and sipped on cucumber juice to keep her skin dewy soft. She skipped to her favorite part of the story, where the wicked hag is rolled down a hill in a nail-spiked barrel, until all that remains is her bracelet made of little boys' bones. Gazing at the gruesome bracelet, Sophie felt her thoughts drift to cucumbers. Suppose there were no cucumbers in the woods? Suppose other princesses had depleted the supply? No cucumbers! She'd shrivel, she'd wither, she'd—

Dried melon flakes fell to the page. She turned to the mirror and saw her brow creased in worry. First ruined sleep and now wrinkles. At this rate she'd be a hag by afternoon. She relaxed her face and banished thoughts of vegetables.

As for the rest of Sophie's beauty routine, it could fill a dozen storybooks (suffice it to say it included goose feathers, pickled potatoes, horse hooves, cream of cashews, and a vial of cow's blood). Two hours of rigorous grooming later, she stepped from the house in a breezy pink dress, sparkling glass heels, and hair in an impeccable braid. She had one last day before the School Master's arrival and planned to use each and every minute to remind him why she, and not Belle or Tabitha or Sabrina or any other impostor, should be kidnapped.